Excitement Flooded Her Veins.

Caitlin was here—in Tumbleweed, Texas, miles from her doting, smothering parents and a world away from the restrictions and restraints she'd known all her life. Soaking up the atmosphere, she renewed her silent vow to change her life.

She watched as a cowboy swaggered in. He stood not quite six feet tall, with broad shoulders and long legs. With a lazy arrogance, he surveyed the room as if he owned it and everything inside. When he connected with Caitlin, his gaze locked with hers. Knowing she ought to break eye contact, she found she simply couldn't. Fascinated by the man, she let her gaze linger. Her skin tingled slightly; her breathing grew faint. For the first time in twenty-four years, she became conscious of being a woman, of latent femininity, of desire and an impish longing to match wits with this man....

Dear Reader,

This May we invite you to delve into six delicious new titles from Silhouette Desire!

We begin with the brand-new title you've been eagerly awaiting from the incomparable Ann Major. *Love Me True,* our May MAN OF THE MONTH, is a riveting reunion romance offering the high drama and glamour that are Ann's hallmarks.

The enjoyment continues in FORTUNE'S CHILDREN: THE BRIDES with *The Groom's Revenge* by Susan Crosby. A young working woman is swept off her feet by a wealthy CEO who's married her with more than love on his mind—he wants revenge on the father who never claimed her, Stuart Fortune. A "must read" for all you fans of Daphne Du Maurier's *Rebecca!*

Barbara McMahon's moving story *The Cowboy and the Virgin* portrays the awakening—both sensual and emotional—of an innocent young woman who falls for a ranching Romeo. But can she turn the tables and corral *him?* Beverly Barton's emotional miniseries 3 BABIES FOR 3 BROTHERS concludes with *Having His Baby.* Experience the birth of a father as well as a child when a rugged rancher is transformed by the discovery of his secret baby—and the influence of her pretty mom. Then, in her exotic SONS OF THE DESERT title, *The Solitary Sheikh,* Alexandra Sellers depicts a hard-hearted sheikh who finds happiness with his daughters' aristocratic tutor. And *The Billionaire's Secret Baby* by Carol Devine is a compelling marriage-of-convenience story.

Now more than ever, Silhouette Desire offers you the most passionate, powerful and provocative of sensual romances. Make yourself merry this May with all six Desire novels—and buy another set for your mom or a close friend for Mother's Day!

Enjoy!

Joan Marlow Golan
Senior Editor, Silhouette Desire

Please address questions and book requests to:
Silhouette Reader Service
U.S.: 3010 Walden Ave., P.O. Box 1325, Buffalo, NY 14269
Canadian: P.O. Box 609, Fort Erie, Ont. L2A 5X3

THE COWBOY
AND THE VIRGIN
BARBARA McMAHON

SILHOUETTE *Desire*

Published by Silhouette Books

America's Publisher of Contemporary Romance

SILHOUETTE BOOKS

ISBN 0-373-76215-1

THE COWBOY AND THE VIRGIN

Copyright © 1999 by Barbara McMahon

This edition published by arrangement with Harlequin Books S.A.

® and TM are trademarks of Harlequin Books S.A., used under license. Trademarks indicated with ® are registered in the United States Patent and Trademark Office, the Canadian Trade Marks Office and in other countries.

Look us up on-line at: http://www.romance.net

Printed in U.S.A.

BARBARA McMAHON

loves to read, write and drink lattes on the porch of a nearby coffeehouse. She has been writing for more than fifteen years for Harlequin and Silhouette and finds it great fun. Living in California's Sierra Nevada, she loves to take long walks in summer and go skiing in winter. Genealogy is a favored hobby she indulges in between books. Fans may write Barbara at P.O. Box 977, Pioneer, CA 95666.

To Jeannette Murakami, a longtime friend
who always stays up late to read my books.
Thanks JM!

One

Caitlin Delany walked boldly toward the door of the Oasis, her first cowboy bar. Garish neon signs lit the crowded parking lot, which formed a garish glow in the dark Texas night. Pickup trucks were parked haphazardly, some dusty and battered, others shiny and new. Few cars were evident.

Loud country music spilled out into the night—a rocking, pumping tune that had her heart skipping in time. She took a deep breath and smiled. Her excitement was mixed with only a hint of trepidation. Tossing back her head, she reached for the door. Shyness and awkwardness didn't have a place on a Friday night in a wild, rollicking country-western bar in Tumbleweed, Texas. She'd made the decision to change her life—this was but one more step in that process. She wanted this. Needed it.

Brazen it out, girl, she admonished as the door swung wide open.

"Are you really ready for this?" Joan asked just behind her.

Caitlin looked over her shoulder at her friend. "Absolutely! Let's go." The wave of music that poured through the open door all but drowned out her voice.

She ignored Joan's look of uncertainty. Joan had done a lot for her, more than she had a right to expect. She wanted to make sure her friend never regretted it. But a Friday evening of fun and dancing in a cowboy bar wasn't going to cause regrets.

Caitlin cruised into the bar like she'd been doing it all her life, instead of for the first time. She was immediately struck by the pounding beat of the band, the milling sea of faces and the thick layer of smoke. Obviously, bars in Texas didn't adhere to the no-smoking rules she was used to. For a second she hesitated—wondering what she was doing. She couldn't afford to get sick. She started her new job on Monday.

Taking a tentative breath, she felt relief flood through her at her lack of reaction to the smoke. Her doctor had been right—she was as healthy as a horse.

She smiled at the simile. Already thinking in the local lingo, she thought proudly. Living in the heart of cattle country for less than a week, she already knew the folks in Tumbleweed related everything to the local economy—cattle, horses, hay.

"There's an empty table," Joan said, pointing as she began to thread her way through the crowd, skirting tables, calling greetings to friends. Caitlin followed as quickly as her new cowboy boots and tight denim jeans permitted. She saw the questioning glances and smiled back, her eyes alight with eager pleasure. Who among these strangers would become friends? What would they find in common? Most wore jeans as she did, but the worn cowboy boots gave proof their occupations differed dramatically from her own. She knew virtually nothing about ranching. And this was a small town. How soon would they accept an outsider?

She could number on one hand the people she already knew—Joan, Mr. Swanson, the principal of the primary school where she would be teaching, and the landlord of her new apartment. It was time she met more people. Weaving around the obstacle course of tables, Caitlin reached the vacant one seconds behind Joan.

"Want a beer?" Joan yelled.

Caitlin nodded as she sat and gazed around, totally fascinated by the scene before her. The music cranked up even louder, the guitars and drum pounding a fast beat. The din made casual conversation next to impossible. An occasional clack of wood-on-wood drew her gaze. Two pool tables stood near the far wall, both encircled by men. Were women not allowed to play?

The stomping on the dance floor caught her attention. Watching the dancers, Caitlin felt excitement flood her veins. She was here—in Tumbleweed, miles from her doting, smothering, lying parents and a world away from the restrictions and restraints she'd known all her life. The men and women crowding the dance floor, sun-bronzed and fit, looked as alien to her as she felt she must look to them. Soaking up the atmosphere, she renewed her silent vows to change her life. Every new experience strengthened her resolve. She had so much catching up to do!

Everywhere she looked, she saw cowboy hats. Black, brown, even an occasional white one. Were those for the good guys, she wondered whimsically. She'd never seen a cowboy hat in Maryland. She'd bought her own jeans and boots on her first morning in Tumbleweed. Maybe a Stetson should be next on her list. She'd go for a black one—so no one would mistake her for a good guy. She'd been good for twenty-four years, and now it was time for her to be a bit bad!

As she scanned the room, her gaze returned to the fast and furious dance steps. Couples circled rapidly, boots stomping, hips swaying, enjoyment shining on their faces.

Caitlin watched enviously. She hadn't a clue how to dance like that. Glancing around, she wondered if she were the only woman in the room who couldn't join in. Probably. For a moment her anger at her parents began to rise. But she forced herself to relax, to ignore the pull toward the quagmire of self-pity. It was over. She was on her own and staying that way!

They had fought her every step, but she was stronger than either of them had expected. Ten days ago she'd discovered the truth. The cost of freedom had been a clean break. She'd packed her bags, cashed in her bonds and left home. And the only way for any kind of equanimity now was to push the anger away. "Live for the Day" was her new motto.

She smiled in gratitude at her friend. Joan had been a lifesaver. They'd been friends in college, both studying to become teachers. If Joan had been surprised at Caitlin's startling revelations on the phone a week ago, she had hidden it well, instantly telling her of a possible job at the local primary school. One of the teachers had just delivered a baby and quit. It was hard to fill jobs in mid-January. Caitlin had applied without hesitation.

The waitress brought them two mugs of beer. "Anything else, ladies?"

"No." Joan slipped her a bill and waved away the change. Raising her mug, she held it toward Caitlin. "To your new life. Live it up, girl, you deserve it."

Caitlin clanked her mug against Joan's and drank. She tried not to wrinkle her nose, not really liking the taste of beer. Was it an acquired taste? Would she like anything else? Living an extremely sheltered existence for twenty-four years didn't lend itself to worldliness. Her parents rarely drank—and they never gave any liquor to their only child.

The music wound down, then stopped. The sudden cessation of noise made conversation possible. Before Caitlin could share her reactions, however, a strange murmur rushed around the room. All eyes turned to the door. She swiveled and watched as two cowboys swaggered in.

There was a definite similarity—both wore Stetsons, faded jeans, boots and plaid shirts. There ended the similarity.

The man on the left demanded her full attention. He stood not quite six feet tall, with broad shoulders and long legs. The aura surrounding him was aggressively male. His skin was darkly tanned, his hair, what she could see below his hat, was dark and maybe a trifle long. With a lazy arrogance, he surveyed the room like he owned it and everything inside.

He must be well-known, Caitlin thought, hearing several people call greetings, which he returned with a careless grin, adding a word or two that brought a laugh from one table.

His smile did strange things to her—blatantly sexy, all-knowing, masculine as hell. She swallowed and watched, mesmerized. He worked the crowd as if he were used to being the center of attention—and liked it.

Caitlin slowly looked around the room. A few men and women regarded him warily—including Joan. Most were laughing, however, at his outrageous remarks and seemed to egg him on. Who was he?

She gazed back at the stranger. He spoke quietly to his companion as his gaze scanned the bar again. When he noticed Caitlin, his gaze locked with hers. For a long moment the two of them stared across the crowded room. Caitlin squirmed slightly in her chair. Knowing she ought break eye contact, she found she simply couldn't. Fascinated by the man, she let her gaze linger. Her skin tingled slightly; her breathing grew faint. Awareness of a sexual nature took hold, filled her. For the first time in twenty-four years she became conscious of being a woman, of latent femininity, of desire and an impish longing to match wits with this man.

Was the attraction purely one-sided? She had read about this, but thought it only fiction. His eyes didn't waver. Did he feel this strange pull of connection?

Slowly he smiled again—lopsided and sexy. He headed straight for her walking across the room as if he didn't even see the other people or the tables and chairs, didn't hear the ribald remarks tossed after him. Smoothly circling obstacles, he never dropped his gaze as he approached, like a wolf on the hunt.

He seemed to gain in stature the closer he came. Caitlin blinked, conscious of the fluttering in her tummy, of the way her heart thudded against her ribs. She drew in a deep breath. Over the smoke and beer, she smelled him, the scent unknown, yet somehow familiar—a scent of leather, hay and a tangy hint of masculinity. She blinked, feeling as tongue-tied as a shy schoolgirl, as hot as a Maryland summer afternoon and about as sophisticated as a five-year-old.

"Care to dance?" The voice was low, husky and sexy—instantly giving rise to thoughts of black velvet, dark nights and tangled sheets.

"Butt out, Zach," Joan said sharply.

Caitlin swung around to her friend, almost surprised to see her there. For several long moments she'd been solely aware of the man standing beside her. She was startled at the animosity in her friend's tone.

"Joan!"

"Sorry, Caitlin, but this guy's not for you." Joan glared at the cowboy. "He's wild and obnoxious and so far out of your league it's not funny."

Instantly Caitlin's ire rose. She'd left home to take charge of her own life, to escape people making her decisions for her. She had resolved never to put up with it from anyone again, friend or foe.

"I think I can decide that for myself," she said tightly.

"Then come on, little darlin'." Zach slipped his hand beneath her arm and helped her to her feet. "It's only a dance, Joan. No need to get all riled up. You can watch every step like an old hound dog." His tone was mocking.

"I don't need a watchdog," Caitlin said, her blood suddenly pounding through her veins. From anger, or from his touch? Nerve endings tingled where his hand gripped, and her knees grew weak. She looked up. He topped her by over half a foot, but that was normal. Almost everyone she knew was taller. At least he didn't tower over her like some men did.

"No one said you did," Joan said distracted. She threw a dark look at Zach. "Leave her alone." She turned to Caitlin. "There are a lot of guys here. I wouldn't trust this one as far as you can throw him."

Zach let his gaze roam insolently down Caitlin's body, then looked at Joan the challenge blatant in his eyes. "The lady looks all grown-up to me. I bet she can take care of herself." Without waiting for a response, Zach turned Caitlin away from the table and headed for the bar.

"The band will be back from break soon, have a drink while we wait. I've been trailing cows all week and worked up a thirst."

"I had a beer," Caitlin said indicating the glass left behind, the one she'd barely touched.

He leaned closer, until she could see the faint lines radiating from his dark blue eyes. Until she could see herself reflected in his dark pupils, feel the heat from his body envelop her.

"Take a chance, darlin', and come with me. I'll get you a fresh one."

Fascinated, Caitlin considered she might just follow him to the ends of the earth, just to hear that voice, to feast her eyes on his rugged features. Boldly she raised her chin and nodded.

"Why not?" Some confusion remained, but for the moment Caitlin felt wildly free—alive as never before. No man had ever taken one look at her and crossed a crowded room just to ask her to dance. Almost giddy with delight, she relished the feelings that crashed through her. Hot thoughts tumbled in her mind. Her body seemed to have developed a will of its own. She couldn't wait to see what happened next. Ten minutes in a bar and she'd already been picked up! She wanted to shout her surprise.

He smiled that sexy smile, his teeth white and even, against the leather brown of his tan. His eyes seem to blaze with some inner light as he let his gaze roam over her face, boldly down her body. She stood taller, wishing she were five-ten instead of five-four. Wishing she had the voluptuous body most men dreamed about, rather than the trim, petite figure she'd had since turning sixteen.

Despite her lack of attributes, the blatant interest in his eyes made her feel sexy, desirable—all woman. Something that would surely shock her mother if she ever found out. Caitlin firmly pushed all thoughts of her parents away, reveling instead in these new sensations.

"New in town?" His voice sent shivers down her back. His mouth was close enough to feel the brush of his breath. Nodding, Caitlin slanted her eyes up toward his, trying to remember everything she'd read about flirting. Could she hold his interest? At least until they'd had a chance to dance?

"I'm Caitlin Delany." She politely held out her hand.

"Zach Haller, darlin'. Glad to meet you." Amusement danced in his eyes as he took her hand in his and held it. And held it.

She wondered if he planned to let it go, then decided she didn't care. The shimmers of excitement that flashed up her arm could hold her enthralled all night. Looking into his eyes, she wondered if she'd seen an emotion deeper than amusement—like interest?

He released her hand, catching up her other one. Threading his fingers through hers, he led Caitlin toward the long, polished mahogany bar.

Cowboys stopped them during the short distance, slapping Zach on the back, asking what trouble he'd been in since they'd last seen him. Several angled for an introduction to Caitlin, which he never made. Confused and fascinated, she watched avidly, taking in every word, trying to discover a clue to understand the code that explained what people talked about. Secretly thrilled at being sought by this man, she vaguely wondered why he didn't introduce her to his friends.

When they reached the bar, he squeezed in between two others, flinging his arm across her shoulders. The length of his hard body pressed against hers. She felt hemmed in, surrounded by him. His mouth came close to her ear again.

"Beer okay, babe?"

Babe! Caitlin's eyes opened wider. No one had ever called her babe. Daringly she leaned slightly against the inviting male chest. She could feel his strength, his tight muscular build. No fat on this man. He wasn't some Saturday-night urban cowboy, but a hard worker, she knew instinctively.

"Beer is fine." She wondered if she would ever find the courage to call a man babe or darlin'.

Zach caught the bartender's eye and held up two fingers. Then he turned his attention back to Caitlin. The intensity of his gaze startled her, as if he blanked out the rest of the room and focused solely on her. Nervous flutters filled her stomach as she boldly held his gaze.

"So, Caitlin Delany, tell me how long you've been in Tumbleweed, where you're from and how well you know that prude Joan Parker?"

Caitlin stiffened and pulled slightly back from him. "Joan and I went to college together. She's my friend."

He shrugged easily. "Don't get bent out of shape. Let's just say Joan doesn't approve of me. But you look like someone who makes her own decisions, reserves judgment.''

Warily Caitlin nodded. ''Does she have reason to disapprove of you?''

He smiled again, his face even closer. Caitlin blinked, suddenly curious to know what his mouth would feel like against hers. She licked her lips, fastening her gaze on that wide smile. His lips were nicely formed. She bet he knew everything there was about kissing a woman. And she was a raw novice—but it didn't stop her raging curiosity.

''Naw. Sometimes I like to cut loose a bit. Joan doesn't approve, but, hell, half the town doesn't approve so that's nothing new.''

Caitlin frowned, who *was* he and what did cutting loose entail?

''You're a cowboy, right? So what outrageous things do you do?''

''Nothing, darlin'. I'm just a hardworking man, who comes to town from time to time for a little relaxation and action—pure as the driven snow.''

''I just bet.'' She wasn't that naive. ''What kind of action are you looking for?''

''Whatever I can find,'' he said, nudging her closer to the bar, pressing against her. His attention focused on her, his eyes traced her face, his hand rested on her shoulder.

''Where do you work?'' She took a deep breath, trying to calm the rioting sensations. People did this kind of thing all the time. It meant nothing. Yet, her senses filled with his pure male scent and her heart rate increased.

''Place called the Lazy H Ranch. Just a few miles north of town. Been in Tumbleweed long?''

''Since Wednesday.''

''Here only three days? Your social life needs establishing, sweets. Ah.'' He turned as the bartender set two mugs of beer on the bar before them.

Raising his mug, Zach inclined it toward Caitlin's.

"Here's to hot times," he murmured taking a deep pull of the brew, his eyes never leaving hers.

Hot times? Her mind conjured up images of searing kisses, petting in the dark; tangled sheets and his husky voice at midnight. She sipped the beer as her imagination ran rampant. What she lacked in actual experience, she made up for in knowledge from hundreds of books.

What would Zach Haller be like to make love to? Hot and fast, she bet. And maybe a lot of fun. She suspected from the irreverent comments he'd made to his friends on the short way to the bar that he took nothing seriously. Including a relationship with a woman, she surmised.

"Drink up. When the band returns, we'll dance, and I'll tell you all about being a Texas cowboy." The amusement was evident as he looked at her.

Was he laughing at her? Taking a determined sip of her beer, she accidentally banged her mug on the bar.

"Do I look young and naive?" she asked boldly. He mocked her, she knew, but his teasing seemed in fun. Oddly holding her own, she felt competent and sophisticated and almost at ease, standing in his half embrace. If her rioting senses would only settle down enough to let her think. She'd never been held like this, casually, yet possessively. And she'd never felt so on edge, as if on a precipice. One wrong step, would she crash over?

"Absolutely, little Caitlin Delany. You look incredibly young and wide-eyed and innocent as hell." He cocked his head slightly, the dark Stetson shading his eyes from the overhead lights. "Nice effect."

She blinked. So much for feeling worldly and sophisticated. He certainly didn't look young and wide-eyed.

"You know, cowboy, this is just the façade I put on to fool people. I bet I could teach you a thing or two," she drawled provocatively. Then she looked away, flustered. Where had those words come from? Reckless to the point of abandonment, she surprised herself. And felt good.

"I'd love to learn. What do you have in mind?" he murmured, leaning even closer—almost embracing her right at the bar!

"What's left for you to learn, darlin'?" she said, bluffing.

Slowly Zach smiled, setting his almost-empty mug on the counter beside hers. "Not much. Maybe we should run a list and see where we stand, see if anything is missing."

Caitlin sought a sassy answer. He was having fun, she could tell. So was she. The thought almost surprised her. Impishly letting her gaze drop and scan as much of him as she could, she shrugged. "Doesn't seem like anything's missing from my viewpoint."

He laughed, rich and full. People around them turned and smiled. She couldn't help but return their smiles.

The band shuffled back up on the small, makeshift stage. Zach inclined his head. "Ready for that dance?"

Her smile faded as she looked over toward the patch of dance floor. "We don't dance like this in Maryland," she stalled, loath to refuse, yet afraid of making a total idiot of herself.

His arm encircled her waist. "Come on, darlin', time you learned the Texas two-step. I'm a great teacher. I can show you all you need to know."

Ten minutes later Zach knew he was more interested in this woman than he had a right to be. She was light on her feet and quickly learned the steps. He liked the way she looked: her light blond hair; her blue eyes—not as dark as his, but light and starry-eyed. He shook his head and almost laughed. Was the joke on him? Had he truly picked up some innocent young thing? For a moment he almost believed he had.

But he knew people weren't what they appeared on the surface. Knew women especially were devious and underhanded, saying one thing, meaning another. And always looking for the fast buck. Did she think playing a role of an innocent would be the best way to snare an unwary cowboy? Too bad he was too savvy to get caught.

"You were going to tell me all about being a cowboy," she said a moment later. The way she had of slowly raising her eyelids as if she were shy, then boldly gazing straight into his eyes was disconcerting as hell. For a moment Zach felt as if she could see straight through him—through the barriers he raised, through to the depth of feeling he tried so hard to hide.

"What do you want to hear?" He'd be more interested in hearing about Caitlin Delany. Glancing over at Joan, he met her glaring eyes. He smiled and spun Caitlin around. Nothing like getting someone mad to stimulate the senses. For a second he almost felt guilty. Joan Parker had never done anything to him, not like some of the other citizens of Tumbleweed with their gossip and disapproving frowns.

"What do you do all day—ride horses, herd cattle? How did you get to be a cowboy? Is it what you wanted all your life? Did you watch Westerns when you were a kid? What about being a marshall or Texas Ranger? Didn't that appeal to you?" Caitlin rattled off the questions so quickly, he suspected she'd been a fan of Westerns. This was one starry-eyed woman. How much was an act?

He looked into Caitlin's guileless gaze. For a moment he felt another tendril of something move deep inside. She was prettier than most women he saw, with a wholesome air that was oddly tantalizing. Did she realize this and deliberately make it work for her? Or could she possibly be as innocent as she seemed?

No, it had to be an act. He knew women. And she wouldn't have ditched her friend so quickly to dance with a stranger if she was as innocent as she looked.

"I was born on the Lazy H. Ranching is all I do now."

"Now?" She quickly picked up on the word.

He smiled and spun her around, hoping to chase away

the shaft of pain that pierced. Talk about the ranch, not the other. Focus on what he had, not what he'd lost. Entertain her with tall tales and then either let her go, or move on to the next step. Another Friday night to get through. If he had enough beer, it would blur the anguish and drive the memories away.

"A typical day means getting up early, then making sure the working stock is fed, the stalls mucked out. Then depending on what needs doing, I do it. From cleaning tack to riding fence to moving cattle from one section of range to another. Maybe shoeing some horses or cutting hay."

There were always a million things to do on the ranch. Endless chores that stretched out forever. For a moment the bleakness of the future almost took hold. He pushed away the feeling and gazed into her blue eyes. He was here for fun tonight. Not to worry about the years ahead.

"I've never been on a ranch," she confided, looking into his eyes.

He pulled her closer, relishing the feel of her high, firm breasts against his chest, her legs bumping against his as they moved with the tempo. "Somehow that doesn't surprise me. You'll have to come see my place sometime." Maybe even tonight. He'd love to see that blond hair spread out on a pillow, to run his work-roughened hands across that silky skin, to taste her, touch her. Learn her secrets and show her a few of his own. Maybe make up that list they discussed earlier and see who could teach whom what.

"Don't you live in a bunkhouse?"

He laughed and eased back a bit. Her body was too enticing. He felt a growing interest in a certain part of his anatomy that he didn't care to share with the rest of the bar's customers.

"No, I have a small house on the ranch. Not too close to the main house." The only thing that kept him sane, he sometimes thought. He could go home at night and shut the door. Shut out the reality of life.

"If I came, could you teach me to ride?" she asked.

Zach almost groaned as he looked into her blue eyes. Heat spread from his gut. There was no double meaning in her expression, but he thought of how he'd like to teach her to ride, to explore the pleasures they could discover between them, and put a bloom of color in her cheeks from making love. He tightened his grip on her hand, his other hand splayed on her back. He wanted her closer, as close as two people got.

The song ended. He didn't want to let her go.

"That was fun, thank you for asking me to dance," Caitlin said primly as she stepped back.

He tilted her chin up with a finger and brushed his lips across hers. She tasted warm and sweet. And seemed shocked to death if the startled expression in her eyes was anything to go by. A flicker of doubt pricked him. Could she possibly be as innocent as she appeared?

Caitlin cleared her throat, tilted her head to the right. A smile tilted up one side of her mouth. "Is that part of dancing Texas style? Interesting finale."

Slowly smiling in return, he shook his head. He glanced impatiently at the band. Why didn't they start another song?

She licked her lips, and he stifled a soft moan at the surge of feelings that shook him. The woman was lethal!

"Tell me what brings you to Tumbleweed?" he asked, watching the way her mouth moved, wondering when he could really kiss her. Not some little chaste peck on the dance floor, but a full-blown, knock-your-socks-off kiss. With nibbles and tongues and bodies pressed so tightly together they would have trouble knowing where one ended and the other began. He looked over toward the door. They could gain some privacy in the parking lot.

"A job, freedom, a new beginning." The words tumbled out.

"Here?" She made Tumbleweed sound like Mecca. "There are a lot of other places that have jobs. And more going for them than Tumbleweed. This is an old, small town. Freedom is more a dream than reality. Wait until your neighbors think they know more about your life than you do, and feel they have a right to tell you how to live."

"I like Tumbleweed."

"There speaks a person with three days living here behind her. Wait a week or two."

"You live here, don't you like it?"

Despite his best efforts, he felt the familiar tension rise. No, he damn well did not like it. But he clamped down on the anguish the question brought. Smiling to hide the ache, he kept his mask in place. "It's home."

"Which is a nonanswer," she replied, narrowing her eyes as she studied him.

Zach shifted a bit and headed back toward the bar. He didn't need anyone delving into things best left alone. His hand casually linked with hers, she didn't protest. Behind them the members of the band were talking with the customers, trying to find out what songs people wanted to hear.

"It was an answer," he said. All the answer he planned to give.

"No. Calling it home doesn't tell me if you like it or not. I left home because I didn't like it. People don't always like their home."

"So you are making a new start far from home?" he asked.

"I'm making a start, actually. It's exciting and a bit scary. But I'm determined to do this." She tilted her chin pugnaciously, and it was all Zach could do to keep walking and not pull her into his arms and kiss her silly. He frowned. It had been years since anyone had made such a impression on me. Why tonight?

"Hey, Zach, long time no see, cowboy." A sultry redhead sauntered up to them, reached up and kissed him on the mouth. He smiled, encircling her waist with his left hand, still holding Caitlin's hand with his right. He liked being with women—as long as they knew the score. They were soft, smelled good and constantly surprised him. As long as they knew there'd be no lengthy entanglements— no "trusting" for this cowboy—he took the fun where he found it and moved on.

Anita was usually fun, even if she did tend to be a bit possessive.

"Hey, babe, how're things going?" Keep it light, that was his motto.

"Better for seeing you, honey. Where've you been? It's been totally dullsville in town these past couple of weeks."

"Thought I'd try the action in San Angelo, beats this burg."

She pouted and looked at Caitlin, her eyes glittering in the smoky room. "Who's she?"

"Caitlin Delany, meet Anita Black. Caitlin's new in town."

"Visiting, or moving in?" Anita asked.

"I start work Monday at the primary school, I'm a teacher," Caitlin said.

Anita looked at her, at Zach, then burst out laughing. "I don't believe it, Zach Haller making a play for a prim schoolteacher. What a joke!"

Zach smiled the lazy smile he was known for, though inside he wanted to turn around and stalk out of the bar. It figured that Miss Innocence Personified would turn out to be a damned schoolteacher. That would probably make her as big a prude as her friend Joan. What a sucker punch!

"Time I got some more education," Zach said easily. He would play it out, then return the teacher to her table. No harm done.

"Actually, I teach first grade," Caitlin said seriously.

Anita laughed again. "Come on, darling, let's split from here. I can teach you anything you don't already know," she drawled, leaning into Zach.

He raised the hand he'd linked with Caitlin. "Already taken tonight, babe. Maybe a rain check?"

Anita frowned then shrugged. "Sure thing, sugar. By the way, Margot Simmons is gunning for you."

"Margot? Why?"

"I don't know, but I heard she's on the warpath and blasting your name to kingdom come. Watch your step, sugar."

With one more hot kiss, Anita moved away, meeting up with another cowboy she seemed just as friendly with.

Zach noticed Caitlin watching her, obviously fascinated. He became annoyed; he wanted Caitlin's whole attention.

"Is there a rule against cowboys seeing teachers?" Caitlin asked, turning back to him.

"Not in this town."

When the band started a slow melody in the next instant, Caitlin wondered if Zach would want to dance. It seemed that the lights dimmed a bit, but it could have been the cigarette smoke growing thicker. She still felt no discomfort.

Without asking, Zach led her back to the dance floor and looped his arms behind her, pulling her so close every inch touched.

Caitlin resisted for about half a second, then relaxed and molded her body to his, resting her forehead against his cheek, her nose almost pressed against his neck. Excitement grew as his scent filled her. She took a deep breath, imprinting the memory for all time. She was dancing with a sexy cowboy, one who turned down a rather obvious offer from a voluptuous redhead to dance again with her!

Slowly she smiled. Life was getting interesting.

Dancing with Zach was the most erotic thing she'd ever experienced. Of course, with her background that wasn't saying much. But still, she felt gloriously wanton and uninhibited. As they moved around the dance floor, his legs brushed against hers, his thigh came between hers suggestively as they moved in time to the languid beat. Slowly, in tempo, his hands rubbed her back, pressing her against his chest, moving with her hips as they swayed. She tripped, and he tightened his grip.

Caitlin had difficulty breathing. And when she did, all she could smell was Zach Haller. Tendrils of shimmering awareness brushed through her, built as the moments stretched out. Every step raised her temperature another notch. She felt totally feminine, powerful, almost intoxicated, as if she could crook her little finger and bend this virile man to her will. It was a heady idea. He'd turned down the offer for a dance with that sexy redhead. He'd possessively kept her to himself, refusing to even introduce her to his friends at the bar. There had to be some attraction on his part. She had never experienced anything like it.

When his lips brushed her cheek, Caitlin stumbled again. She tightened her arms around his neck, then pulled her head back, gazing into the glittering intensity of his blue eyes. She wanted to see him, implant every feature on her mind as she had every aspect of the night.

Zach closed the scant distance between them and covered her mouth with his. This was no brushing touch. He molded his warm lips to hers, moving persuasively, sending shock waves to the tips of her fingers and toes. When his tongue slowly outlined her lips, her knees threatened to give way. Only the strong wall of his chest and his arms about her kept her upright.

Heart pounding, Caitlin never thought to pull away—too entranced with the sensations that coursed through her. This must be what making love felt like—only more. Captivated by the sheer delight that built inside her, she felt her heated blood pound through her veins. Did Zach feel the same?

Caitlin leaned against the strength of him and opened her mouth in response to his tongue's teasing. She expected a plunging orgy, but instead got tantalizing nibbles. His tongue danced with hers, tasted, retreated as if offering an invitation. Boldly she responded, letting her own tongue tentatively touch his lips, move to the warm moistness behind.

The world spun out of control as Caitlin reveled in sensations that were totally foreign. She had trouble breathing, but didn't care. The slow strains of the music seemed to become a part of her as she and Zach swayed in time, his mouth fused against hers. She greedily sought more of the shimmering pleasure she'd never known existed.

When he ended the kiss, it was to trail his mouth along her jaw to the sensitive lobe of her ear. Gently nipping, he immediately soothed with his tongue. Caitlin felt as if she'd run a marathon. Her heart pounded so hard she knew Zach had to feel it. Her skin felt so sensitized she thought she would burst. Against her belly she could feel the hard arousal that she'd only read about. And the flush of blood pumping wildly through her veins had her longing for cool air.

This man wanted her! Shocked, she opened her eyes.

"Come home with me, Caitlin. I'll show you the ranch," Zach murmured in her ear, still swaying to the soft beat of the music.

She couldn't believe he remained on his feet, much less had the wherewithal to keep dancing. Pulling back a bit, she gazed deeply into his eyes. Her heart fluttered, her throat grew tight, as she slowly slid her gaze to his lips. Licking her own, she wondered if he tasted her as she still tasted him.

"Is that the same thing as come up and see my etchings?" she asked huskily.

Two

He laughed. "Only if that's a line you want to hear."

Flushing slightly, Caitlin tossed her head, determined she would never reveal her lack of experience to this cocky cowboy. Tonight was special—she had never had so much fun! She felt free and wild, daring and bold. She had spent her entire life waiting for this. She planned to soak up every second.

Flirting up at him, she smiled. "Maybe more than you think, cowboy."

Her mother would die if she saw her daughter flirting with this man. It seemed glaringly obvious he had more experience in his little finger than Caitlin had ever had. But the thought only goaded her into making up for lost time. Relishing every moment spent with him, she felt daring enough to flirt.

For a second she grew annoyed that she had even considered stepping away to avoid the dangerous pull of attraction. But was she ready for anything more than a light flirtation? She'd just met the man. Been picked up in a cowboy bar, no less. Her delight in the situation continued to grow. How many daydreams had featured some dashing hero sweeping her off her feet? Just because she had not expected a cowboy didn't mean she shouldn't take advantage of the adventure. And how dangerous could Zach be? So far he'd done nothing but tease her.

And kiss her senseless.

The music came to an end. Reluctantly Caitlin slid her arms down from his neck, her hands skimming over his hard chest. The heat beneath the cotton of his shirt almost scorched her. She hated to break contact. Her legs shaky, she backed up a step. And felt as if a part of herself was missing. She liked being held by Zach.

Joan appeared at her side, grabbed her arm. "Come with me to the ladies' room," she said to Caitlin, avoiding Zach's amused eyes.

He looked at Joan, then Caitlin. The challenge was obvious in his gaze, she thought, flustered at Joan's obvious attempt to separate them.

"I'll be back," she said, and turned to follow Joan to the ladies' room.

"God, Caitlin, are you crazy? I know you're new in town, but even someone as sheltered as you should be able to spot a man like Zach Haller," Joan said as soon as the outer door closed behind them.

Glancing around, Caitlin noticed she and Joan were alone in the room. Through the walls she could still hear the muffled music of the band. Peering into the mirror, she stopped in shock. Her eyes were bright and sparkling. Her hair looked a bit mussed, had Zach run his fingers through it during their kiss? She couldn't remember. Her lips were pink and slightly swollen. Licking them, she tasted Zach again. Her heart thumped in her chest.

Joan rounded on Caitlin, her dark eyes snapping. "Zach Haller has been in more trouble than anyone else in town.

Probably more than all the rest put together. His own father knew he was a wild one and made sure he left the ranch to his brother, Sam, to keep Zach in line. Stay away from him, or you'll be burned so bad you won't know what hit you.''

Caitlin blinked. "He seems—" *Nice* was definitely not the word to use for Zach Haller. But she couldn't come up with one that defined him. Not *dangerous*—or only dangerous in the sense that he could make her forget herself and her sheltered upbringing and yearn for a bright freedom that she had only imagined in the past.

Joan groaned softly. "Caitlin, I know the man looks like a dream, but he can't be trusted at all. He's cocky and crazy and cares for nothing. He was a wild and troublesome teenager, and since he's been back, nothing's changed. I know he can flirt hot enough to put everyone else to shame, but that's not reason enough to lose your head. Stay away from him.''

"Back from where?" Caitlin focused on those words as she turned to face Joan. He had never answered her earlier question about liking Tumbleweed. Had he left to try somewhere else and found Tumbleweed called him home?

"Air Force. He was a jet jockey for a few years."

"That figures," she murmured remembering his don't-give-a-damn, cocky attitude.

"What?" Joan asked.

"He's got that same air of arrogance that I used to see with those cadets at the Naval Academy. Must be something they breed into military men."

"Zach was cocky enough as a teenager, no one needed to breed anything. And now he's even worse."

"Worse? In what way?" Caitlin found herself fully intrigued. Had she just been dancing with the town's bad boy? A small thrill shivered through her as she remembered how he'd cut her out of the crowd. She almost laughed.

They were poles apart, yet he'd come on to her like she was someone special.

"Just worse," Joan said, frustration coloring her tone.

"How?" Caitlin's curiosity rose.

Joan frowned. "I don't know, but he's always being talked about. Of course there's that scandal with his brother, so some of Zach's behavior might be excused. Not that he's the kind of man you should associate with. Caitlin, you don't begin to have the kind of experience you need to hold your own with Zach Haller."

"I still want to know what he does that's so bad. I've never known a bad-boy type before. What scandal?"

"Honestly!" Joan shook her head and paced around the small room. "I'm not getting into that. Don't get any romantic ideas. He's been burned once by a woman and doesn't trust our gender any farther than he can throw it. And he doesn't care about anything. Everything rolls off his back. He takes nothing seriously, so don't go looking for any kind of relationship with him. He's a solo act, Caitlin. The love 'em and leave 'em type. Stay away from him!"

"We're only dancing," she said soothingly. Brushing back her hair, she glanced in the mirror briefly, intrigued with the change she saw in her face. She looked more alive than she'd ever seen herself, glowing with health and happiness.

"And kissing. I couldn't believe it when I saw that," Joan grumbled, glaring at her friend.

Heat stole into Caitlin's cheeks. "Well, that was a bit unexpected." Dare she share the wonder of her feelings with Joan?

"Unexpected my foot. A few more minutes and I wouldn't be surprised to see him strip off your clothes and make love to you on the dance floor."

"Now you're being ridiculous, Joan. It was a kiss. And

you know what? I liked it.'' Caitlin tilted her head proudly, fascinated by the woman in the mirror.

"I'm sure you did. He's got a great reputation for pleasing anyone who goes out with him. And that's, of course, almost any woman he asks. But the man has no staying power."

"There's no harm done, Joan. I'm enjoying myself. And we aren't even going out, just sharing a couple of dances in a room jammed with people."

"No harm! Honestly, Caitlin, you're as innocent as a baby. Your mother will be horrified! I promised her—'' Joan stopped suddenly, her expression stricken.

"You promised my mother what?'' Caitlin asked in a deadly calm voice. She turned from the mirror to stare at the woman who had offered to help her, a sinking feeling in the pit of her stomach.

"Nothing. Caitlin, I'm sorry. I shouldn't have said that."

"I think you need to explain, Joan. What did you promise my mother?''

Joan twisted her fingers together and looked away, then back at Caitlin. Biting her lower lip, she drew in a shaky breath. "Your parents are worried about you, Caitlin. You've never lived away from home, never been out on your own. They wanted to make sure you're all right.''

"Joan, what did you promise?'' Caitlin wanted to shake the answer from her friend, but kept still, hiding the growing anguish that threatened to choke her—for all the lost years, for the experiences she should have had as a teenager, a young adult. Firmly she pushed it away.

"That I'd keep an eye on you, that's all. Let them know how you're doing. Make sure you didn't get into anything over your head. And Zach is definitely in that category. Oh, Caitlin—''

The truth struck Caitlin like a blow.

"No! Listen to me, Joan, and listen carefully. I trusted you. Of all the people I know, you knew what I've gone through. I told you of the lies and the manipulation. I'm twenty-four years old and have lived under my parents' smothering protection every single day of my life until a week ago."

"Caitlin, they love you. They want the best for you."

"It's a sick kind of love when a child cannot be allowed to grow and develop, isn't allowed any freedom." Caitlin was almost too furious for words. Her delight in her new life shattered. She thought things were different, that she was making decisions on her own, but had Joan been acting as a substitute for her parents?

Apparently Zach Haller was the only honest thing that had happened to her since moving to Tumbleweed. And for him she was merely a novelty—the new kid in town. He'd grow bored with her before the evening ended. What she found the most exciting night of her life probably was nothing out of the ordinary for him.

"I'm sorry you've been inconvenienced by my mother. When you report in, please make sure she knows our friendship has ended. I am fighting for my life and can't allow you or them to interfere," Caitlin said slowly. Her perfect evening ended. Back to reality.

"Caitlin, don't. I'm on your side, really. I just felt so bad for your mother when she called. I had to tell her I'd keep an eye out. Don't do anything foolish. Not to get back at me. Stay away from Zach. There are a lot of good guys out there. Dance with some of them…meet different cowboys…go slowly. I don't want something disastrous to happen. You'll leave, then."

"I have no plans to leave. I want to make a home here, at least for the foreseeable future. I've got a job, a nice apartment. You're right, now I need to make a few friends. Ones I can trust." Caitlin was almost shaking with anger. Was there no one on the face of the earth she could trust? No honesty anywhere? What about Zach?

Reality check—she wasn't some femme fatale to entice

men into wild romantic gestures. She couldn't even move out from home without her parents enlisting someone to act as a spy.

Hurt, angry and frustrated, Caitlin turned away from Joan. Time to go and meet other citizens of Tumbleweed, to start building relationships. But she wouldn't forget to watch her back. She no longer trusted Joan. Nor her parents. Anger sustained her. Rebellion surged. She thought she'd made a clean break ten days ago when she'd headed her car west. Apparently not. Her determination to do so strengthened. She'd been dictated to long enough. She would make her own decisions now. Starting tonight!

Caitlin left the rest room. The band was playing a fast tune, and when she looked at the dance floor, she spotted Zach dancing with a woman she had not seen before. Resolutely looking away, Caitlin moved to the table. Her beer remained in the mug. She sipped it and wrinkled her nose. It was warm and growing flat, tasting worse than ever. What she'd really like was a cola.

"Hey, you're Joan's friend, aren't you?" A lanky cowboy stood by the table, grinning down at Caitlin, twisting his hat in his hands.

Caitlin smiled up at the stranger. "I sure am, Caitlin Delany. I just moved to town three days ago."

"Care to dance, ma'am?" he asked.

No magic spark arced between them, but he looked nice, and it beat sitting at the table as if she was waiting for Joan to join her. Or waiting for Zach.

"I'd be delighted," Caitlin replied, hoping he could not tell her heart wasn't in it. He just wasn't a to-die-for man like some other cowboy she'd danced with. She stood up, thrusting Joan's betrayal behind her, refusing to think about it or her parents anymore tonight. She had too much lost time to make up for.

The excitement and delight in the evening had evaporated when Joan confessed she was spying on behalf of her parents. Dancing with a stranger no longer held the same kind of appeal. Maybe she should leave. She was still debating when Zach cut in.

Caitlin tried to squelch the surge of happiness that swept through her when she realized Zach had moved in again. She thanked the cowboy and turned to match her steps with Zach's.

"Dangerous thing, dancing with me now," he said as they moved around the small dance floor in the fast Texas two-step.

"Joan did mention I should watch myself. But then, I already knew that," she said, smiling up into his face.

Amusement lurked in his eyes. "I bet she did more than just warn you."

Caitlin shrugged. "Tell me, are you as bad as she says?"

"Probably. How bad is that?"

Laughing, Caitlin glanced around the crowded dance floor. "Just a warning to expect nothing. Which suits me, because I don't want to get tied down. This is fun and that's all I'm after."

"Girl after my own heart," he said.

Caitlin spotted Joan dancing with a man she didn't recognize. He'd arrived shortly after Joan had returned to the table and monopolized her. She didn't seem to mind, and Caitlin was grateful to have Joan's attention elsewhere. She was determined to have a good time.

Zach was conscious of others watching them dance, no doubt wondering what he was doing. What had Joan told her? Nothing too good if the glaring looks she cast across the dance floor were any indication. Another time he might have been angry at her interference. But not tonight. If Caitlin wanted to dance with him, she could decide for herself. Joan had had her say. And it looked as if Caitlin had ignored her. Showed how new she was in town.

Dancing with her earlier had only whet his appetite for

this babe in grown-up clothing. Something about her roused his curiosity. When he teased her, her eyes would widen slightly, then the most delightful smile spread across her face. Zach was surprised at the heat that smile invoked. He thought himself immune to those kind of feelings around women.

When the band took another break, Caitlin raised one foot and rotated it. "I've never danced so much in my life. My feet hurt, actually. It may be the new boots. I'm going to have to stop soon, and I wanted to close the place down!"

He grinned. "Still can. Take a break, we've got all night. I could teach you pool. We can play that for a while, even after the band returns, if you like."

"Oh, cowboy, pool's one thing I could probably teach you. If you really want to play, I'm game."

"Know how?"

She nodded. "Probably the only game I do know," she murmured as she started across the room.

Her enthusiasm was refreshing, but unexpected. She gave him a sunny smile and almost skipped across the dance floor. He followed, watching her hips sway as she led the way. Rounded and firm, they tantalized him in a most unsettling manner. He needed to be in charge, not his hormones.

Racking the balls, she turned and picked out a cue. "Me first or you?"

"Ladies first," he said. She looked as pleased as punch standing by the table—feminine and sweet. Too sweet? He reached for a cue, wishing instead he could pull her closer and swing her into another dance—one of those slow ones like earlier, where every inch of her body pressed against his. Her laughter filled his ears—lilting, provocative. She hit the white ball and cleanly broke the triangle. One striped ball teetered on the edge of a pocket.

"Six in," she said, lining up the shot. The white ball kissed the other and sent it spinning into the pocket.

"Fun?" He liked looking at the curves in the snug jeans when she leaned over to line up another shot. He wouldn't mind a bit if she had a run that lasted the entire game as long as he could keep an eye on that rounded bottom.

"This whole night is the most fun I've had in forever," she said breathlessly, lining up another ball.

Glancing over to her table, he noticed Joan wasn't there. Had she left? He searched the room.

"Looking for someone?" Caitlin asked after another successful shot.

"Your watchdog," he murmured.

"Forget Joan," she said with a hint of temper. The flash of anger in her eyes surprised him. So the new schoolteacher and her friend weren't any longer on the best of terms. Sudden, wasn't it? Because of the talk in the ladies' room? His curiosity grew.

"So you're a pool hustler in your other life?" he asked.

Caitlin smiled smugly. "Could be, cowboy."

She moved to his side of the table, eyeing the balls. Her sweet fragrance filled his nostrils and sent a shaft of desire straight to his loins. Tightening his hold on the cue stick, he wished he could mold her body against his, revel in the softness of her breasts, the firm muscles of her thighs. For a moment he envisioned pressing his naked body against hers, feeling the pebble push of her nipples, the strength of those thighs wrapped around his waist. Desire flared, and he knew the exact moment she recognized what was happening. She glanced over at him, her eyes darkening and her mouth tightening. A hint of color stained her cheeks, and she whipped around to stare at the table. Zach smiled grimly. Thrust and parry in a game as old as time. Unless he misread the signs, the lady was his for the taking.

Caitlin frowned as she felt the heat washed up into her cheeks. Damn, she didn't need to telegraph her response to the world, especially not to Zach Haller, who would use every bit of persuasion to get his way. She shifted her gaze from Zach's magnetic pull and tried to focus on the game. Her blood felt hot and heavy as it pulsed through her veins. Excitement and daring exploded inside as she tried to ignore the proximity of the male body that inflamed her every cell. She had never experienced anyone so blatantly sexy in her life. She felt free and wild and as wise as an ancient woman. Her awareness of her own sensuality heightened.

Shy, naive Caitlin Delany was desired by this outrageously sexy cowboy.

Heart racing, blood rushing through her head, her hearing faded as only the sound of her pounding pulse filled her.

She drew in a ragged breath, trying to concentrate on her next shot. How many hours had she and her father played pool? Hours when she would have preferred to be hanging out at a mall with friends, or dating, or dancing. Instead, cosseted to the extreme by her parents, she spent her teen years confined to a sterile house, the only activities nonstrenuous ones like pool.

She turned her head to tell him she needed space, but his lips were there, capturing hers, driving every cognizant thought from her mind. She was wrapped in shimmering light, in blazing heat, in pounding sensation. Her body came alive as never before. Her mind clearly saw rainbows and stars, and every breath she took imprinted his scent forever.

When Zach pulled back, Caitlin made to follow him. Wanton desire filled every cell. She had never thought a body could feel so attuned to another. Ready to kick over the traces and explore new limits, she gazed up at him not caring if the hunger showed. Not caring that they were in a bar full of people. She felt rebellious and untamed. She'd been denied so much in life, could she deny herself tonight?

"Babe, you're causing a meltdown," he murmured softly, for her ears alone. "Ready to leave?"

"Leave?" She feasted on his eyes, the blue as deep as the sky over Texas in the early morning. Faint lines crinkled from the corners, his lashes long and dark. The light was dim in the bar, the smoky haze bluish-white as it drifted around. His Stetson shadowed his face so that she could see very little beyond the blaze of blue that stared into her own eyes.

"Did you drive here?" Zach asked, bending closer, wrapping her in the warmth of his body.

Caitlin shook her head. "Joan drove."

"We'll find her and tell her I'll take you home."

Caitlin smiled, butterflies high-kicking in her tummy. "My place or yours?" she whispered, shocked at her boldness. Defiantly she looked around for Joan. She would not be dictated to by her parents, nor her friend. For one night she wanted what other women had, the right to explore her own sensuality—to become secure in that sensuality. Wanted to prolong as long as possible the wild feelings that surged through her.

"You live here in town?"

She nodded.

"Then your place is closer." He brushed his lips across hers again, and Caitlin closed her eyes. He tasted like beer and smoke and man. His lips were hot, moving with expertise as he molded his mouth to hers.

Heart pounding faster than ever, Caitlin nodded. Breaking contact, she smiled up, feeling dreamy and floating. "My place, then." Wordlessly she laid the cue across the table.

Quickly Zach scanned the room. He spotted Joan dancing with a cowboy named Trevor and made a motion with his hand toward Caitlin. Trevor nodded indicating he understood.

"I'll need to tell Joan," Caitlin said, scanning the dance

floor. Good manners dictated that, though she didn't look forward to hearing any more censure from her friend.

"I let her partner know I'll take you home."

"In cowboy code?" she asked, narrowing her eyes.

He smiled, and her insides melted. His teeth were white and even, and the way his mouth moved had her instantly forgetting Joan and good manners. She loved the way he smiled.

"Come on, sugar, show me where your place is."

A night of firsts, Caitlin thought as she scrambled up into the cab of the big pickup truck, when Zach opened the driver's door. He came in right after her as she scooted to the center of the wide seat. Settling in behind the wheel, he started the engine, reaching for her hand. Threading his fingers through hers, he rested their linked hands on his thigh, slowly rubbing against the soft denim material. She couldn't believe she was doing this, inviting a man she'd known only a few hours to her place.

First time in a cowboy bar. First time being picked up. First time dancing for hours and enjoying herself so much. First kiss with a stranger. And first time taking a man home with her. Swallowing hard, she brushed her damp palm over her jeans, gripping his hand tightly with her other.

Yet why not? She was on her own. It was past time to take charge of her life. And she would show her parents and their local spy that she was more than capable of making her own decisions. The sensuous feelings Zach fanned to life had a lot to do with it, too, she admitted.

For an instant panic struck. Had she lost her mind? She hardly knew Zach Haller. Joan didn't approve of him. He was obviously a lady-killer, witness the women who'd been more than willing to dance with him all night, flirting like experts. And that Anita woman who'd kissed him so provocatively.

"Relax, schoolteacher. We're not going to do anything you don't want," Zach said, flicking a quick glance in her direction. "If you want me to drop you at the door, that's fine."

Caitlin smiled and relaxed a bit. A clever man this cowboy. Bent on seduction he knew relaxation would go further with some tense virgin. Heat bloomed at the thought of seduction. How many love scenes had she read in the novels she devoured? Could she bluff her way through the night?

Expectations weren't always met the first time, she tried to warn herself.

For a moment she let her imagination go. Hot kisses, wild caresses, the final act. She knew what he meant about meltdown; she thought she'd burn up if they didn't reach her apartment soon.

She directed him to her street. When he pulled to a stop before the huge Victorian house, he shut off the engine and looked at the place.

"You own this house?" he asked in disbelief.

She shook her head, a jillion nerves screaming inside. "It's been cut up into four apartments. Mine is one of the two upstairs. Come on and I'll show you."

Caitlin loved her apartment. She'd known instantly upon seeing it that it would be perfect. With high ceilings and huge windows, it was light and airy. While small, with only a living room, a kitchen with a small nook for eating, a bedroom and bath, it suited her to a T. She still had loads of decorating to do, but she'd found some bargain furniture her second day in Tumbleweed, so she had made a start.

"I like the porch," Zach said as they climbed the three shallow steps that led to the wide, wraparound porch. Rockers and gliders lined the front of the house. Around the side hung an old-fashioned porch swing.

"It's nice. I'm glad I found it," Caitlin whispered.

"Is it a secret?" Zach whispered back.

"No." She opened the wide front door and stepped inside. A small wattage light dimly illuminated the stairs to the second floor. Two rich mahogany doors stood on either side of the small lobby, obviously leading to the ground-floor apartments.

"But I have neighbors I don't want to waken," she said as she led the way up the wide, wooden stairs.

Zach followed, his boots sounding loud in the hushed night.

"Shh." Caitlin turned and found herself on a level with him. He paused and smiled, tipping back his hat a bit and moving his gaze across her face, stopping at her lips.

"Do that again," he said in a soft voice.

"Shh?" Before she could finish the gesture, he pressed his lips on hers.

"Just right."

Caitlin turned and almost ran up the remaining stairs. Opening her door, she entered first, her heart fluttering. Had she made a mistake? She hadn't a clue what to do next.

"Nice place," Zach said when she switched on a lamp. He moved to her side. "But I didn't come to see your place." He turned her away from the lamp, tossed his hat on the sofa and bent his head to kiss her.

For a moment she was grateful. She didn't have to know what to do, Zach would know. There were just the two of them, alone, in the quiet of her apartment. And his mouth was devastating. He kissed her softly, growing in passion and intensity until she felt as if she floated outside her own body, awash in a flood of sensual feelings.

When his tongue traced the soft sides of her cheeks, she shyly brushed against it with her own, following back into his mouth to explore. She couldn't describe the excitement that filled her; words would never do justice to the overload on her senses. It was heady, provocative and wonderful. She couldn't believe she'd waited twenty-four years to experience a man's passionate kiss.

When he caressed her, she moaned softly in her throat, her skin sensitized to his touch.

"Which way to the bedroom, Caitlin?" he asked softly, his lips trailing fire across her cheeks, nibbling her earlobe, sending sparks of lightning through her. His hands brushed against her breasts, settled on her waist as he held her closer.

Warning bells clamored in her mind, but she ignored them. She had never felt this way before and might never feel this way again. A once-in-a-lifetime event. How often did sexy cowboys cut her away from the rest of the group and want to brand her as his forever? How else to show her parents, to show Joan, to show *herself* she was truly in charge of her future.

"Please," she murmured, her own mouth tasting the skin on his jaw, feeling the slight abrasion of his beard, tasting sunshine and aftershave and Zach Haller. For a novice, she knew she was holding her own when her fingers began to unfasten his shirt. She slid them between the buttons, brushing his hard chest with the backs of her fingers, then slipping the buttons from the holes.

Spreading his shirt, she looked at the broad expanse of tanned chest, with its light dusting of dark hair around his flat nipples. Swallowing hard at the masculine beauty before her, Caitlin lightly danced her fingertips across that expanse. Emboldened by his harsh inhalation, she leaned forward, placing her opened mouth against the tantalizing pectoral muscle. Tasting him with her tongue, she rasped it across that heated skin. His hands came up hard in her hair, pulling her face back and covering her mouth with his in a fiery kiss.

For a brief flash, Caitlin felt wonder. She was not her mother's protected child anymore. Zach Haller made her feel more of a woman than she ever had, and it was glorious.

When his hands tugged at her blouse, she moved one hand to the buttons to unfasten it. Her other hand couldn't leave his chest, her fingers rubbing against the tight muscles, reveling in his heat, in the strength of the man. She'd never touched a man in such a provocative way and couldn't stop.

The feel of the roughened skin from his palms against her sensitized nipples caused an involuntary groan. Her knees almost buckled as heat and desire churned in her center. Opening her eyes, she was shocked at the blaze of blue that gazed down on her. The light seemed too harsh. Why had she turned on the lamp?

Slowly Zach lowered his head until his hot lips covered one rosy nipple. He lapped softly against the pebbled nub, sucking gently, then more fiercely. Caitlin clutched his head, holding him even closer as the waves of pure delight crashed over her, through her, around her.

In a sweeping motion, he bent and picked her up. "Which way to your bed?"

She threw her arms around him, burying her face against the side of his neck. "Through that short hall," she murmured, trying to identify the different feelings that churned through her. She'd never felt this way before. But if this was what she'd been missing, she thanked Joan fervently for playing spy. The discovery had been just what she needed to push her over the edge.

Zach didn't bother with a light when he found the bedroom. He was able to make out the bed from the available illumination. He set Caitlin on her feet and again captured her mouth. He kissed her as if he couldn't get enough of her. Slowly he let his hands move across her satiny skin, learning the feel of her, skimming over her shoulders, down her slim arms, across her plump breasts. He wanted to devour her, but forced himself to move slowly. Something about her cautioned him to hold off on the wild and raw drive that threatened to overwhelm him. There was time enough. All night.

"You unpack any protection yet?" he murmured, his lips

caressing the softness of her neck, feeling the wild pounding of her pulse at the base of her throat.

"Protection?" she asked, freezing up.

He lifted his head and sought her eyes. The light was dim, but he could see them wide open and staring at him.

"I don't have anything with me. Do you?"

She shook her head, looking shocked. She had never even thought about it.

"Damn." He kissed her and then gently set her back. "I'll look in the truck. Maybe I have something in the glove compartment. If not, I'll have to find an all-night drugstore."

"It'll probably be all right."

"Not good enough, Caitlin. I never take chances on something like this. We have all night, right?"

She nodded.

"Kids deserve to be loved into being. Planned for and wanted. Not the result—"

He could see the flush stain her cheeks. "Not the result of a one-night stand, right?" Her voice cracked.

Damn, if he didn't have something in the truck, would she let him back inside if he had to find a store?

"Come with me." He took her hands and tugged. She followed him toward the front door, stopping as she realized her blouse was completely open.

"I can't go out like this."

"Too bad, you look cute."

She hastily fumbled with the blouse, then followed him to the truck. Frustration drove Zach as he plowed through the paraphernalia in the glove compartment. At the bottom—two foil-wrapped packages. Thank goodness. He wasn't sure he could wait if he had to find a store to buy them.

Less than five minutes later he had them both in her bed, clothes discarded where they fell. His hands moved over her skin, marveling at its softness, the satiny smoothness that contrasted so much with his own tough skin. The warmth that captured him came unexpectedly. Her scent filled his mind and he felt himself going slowly crazy with wanting her.

"Caitlin, you're so soft," he whispered as his fingers moved across her thigh, relishing every tantalizing inch he touched.

He moved his hand up her sleek body, leaning over to kiss her cheek, then trailed kisses down her neck, resting his lips on the pulse point at the base of her throat. It pounded rapidly. Her heat raised his own temperature. He wanted her like he'd never wanted anyone.

Her hands drove him wild, lightly caressing, touching like he was something extraordinary. He was about to explode, but couldn't get enough of her. He captured one taut nipple in his mouth again. He rolled his tongue around the tight bud, sucked against her and felt her hips move in ancient reaction. He always insisted on using a condom. But tonight, for a moment, he rebelled. He wished he could feel every inch of her, with nothing in the way. He was going crazy.

Reaching over for the foil packet, he felt as if he were a randy teenager again, trying to score. He had not been this hard the last time he'd slept with a woman. But then, no one else had driven him to the edge so quickly.

Ready in only a moment, he rolled back and gathered her in his arms, pressing her body against his. Her hold was tight, as if she wanted him as much as he wanted her.

Her mouth sought his, claimed his. Her hands molded his back, traced his muscles, his spine, slipped down to press into his hips. Without another word, he turned her on her back, moved between her thighs and pushed home.

"Oh!"

Her cry shocked him. Almost as much as the unbelievable discovery that she was a virgin!

Three

Caitlin felt the hesitation. She tightened her legs around him and opened her eyes, wishing there was more light.

"Don't stop," she whispered.

He surged into her again and again, faster and faster until she felt as if a whirlwind had captured her and spun her higher and higher. After the slight sting of penetration, her body froze for a moment, then eased while the shimmering waves of anticipation began to rebuild.

Flying, she wondered how much more the night could hold. With a cry, she felt the pulsating waves of sheer pleasure sweep through her and carry every thought from her mind except the intense delight.

Zach gave a groan and held still. She could feel a pulse deep within her and tried to imprint every detail on her mind. Never had she expected making love to be so glorious. Could it last forever? Time seemed suspended, thinking was impossible. Her only reality was feeling—feeling the heat that spread, feeling the convulsions that drove her, feeling the hot body that pressed her into the mattress, feeling the sensations of a lifetime.

Slowly everything faded, as she became aware of where she was, who was with her. His body lay across hers, hot and slick. She didn't want to move, except to track random patterns across his muscular back. She liked this feeling—closeness, intimacy. Like floating, almost. Dreamy and delightful. It should have shocked her to be so connected with a stranger, but somehow it felt right.

Slowly Caitlin smiled in triumph. She was a woman now. Her own woman. Answering to no one else.

"Are you all right?" Zach asked, his voice husky in her ear.

"Umm-hmm." She could drift in this afterglow all night. Except she probably wouldn't stay awake that long. Even now her mind seemed fuzzy, her eyes remained closed. Sleep beckoned.

"Caitlin, you should have told me." He pulled back, rolled to the side of the bed.

She nodded, too tired to even speak. She liked hearing his husky voice in the dark of the night. It still reminded her of black velvet, damp tangled sheets and wonders unknown before.

"I'm not for fairy-tale romances and happily-ever-after," he almost growled.

She opened her eyes and tried to see him in the dark. "Did I say I thought you were?" she asked. Suddenly she felt chilled.

"God, I don't know. You're young, naive, and until fifteen minutes ago, a virgin. If you're looking for hearts and flowers now, it's too late. I'm not interested."

The mood shattered. She had not expected anything beyond experiencing a wild and wonderful night. But she sure didn't want to discuss it! Vaguely she felt there should have been more. Something different. But what?

"Maybe you'd better leave," she murmured, yanking the

sheet over her naked body and rising up on her elbow to glare at the man. "I think we both got what we wanted out of tonight. Why don't you get dressed and head for your ranch?"

Zach scowled at her. "What do you mean, we both got what we wanted?"

"You wanted me for a one-night stand, right?" she said, sitting up, the sheet clutched to her breasts, though the absurdity of it hit her. He'd seen her, touched her, tasted her, why bother with modesty now. Nevertheless, she made sure she was covered. "You wanted that from the first moment you saw me in the bar. Well, you got it. And I wanted to live dangerously. I've never been picked up before. I wanted to see what it was like." And thumb her nose at her parents. She knew they'd hear of tonight through Joan. She pushed away the rising anger.

"So we're even, you used me, I used you." He sounded mad.

"If you like." She refused to acknowledge the tawdry feeling his comment gave. It was over, and she had to let go. She had expected something more, but there was nothing. He needed to leave now, not in the morning, when dreams would have had time to weave their magic, and she might voice her disappointment, her vague expectations.

Zach growled something, rose from the bed and found his clothes. He headed for the bathroom. Silhouetted by the light coming into the room from the hall, Caitlin could see his sleek body. She regretted his leaving. She wished he had held her in his arms and—

And what, declared undying love? scoffed a voice in her mind.

No, but she wasn't certain his leaving was what she wanted. She wished he would stay. If he did, would he take her in his arms again and make love to her a second time? There was a second condom. And she wasn't sure she remembered every moment. Everything had been so unexpected, she wanted to find out if it had been a fluke, or if she could experience those feelings again. Find the missing pieces, feel whole and complete and fully a woman.

She wondered if she'd done the right thing in insisting he leave. If he stayed, could they talk a bit? Learn more about each other? Find out if they had interests in common? Find something that would bind them together?

Her grip on the sheet tightened. Foolish thoughts. What would a sexy cowboy have in common with an inexperienced, virginal schoolteacher? And he'd made it more than clear he wanted no ties. Tilting her head in the dark, she raised her chin. She didn't want ties, either!

Zach stepped back into the doorway, fully dressed. He looked at her and then scowled. "Are you all right?" he asked again.

"I'm fine. It was very nice," she said politely.

"Nice! Hell." He spun around and stalked down the hall.

"Goodbye," she said softly. Her ears tracked his movement into the living room—to pick up his hat no doubt. The soft click of the front door let her know he was gone.

Sighing, Caitlin slowly lay back down. Her sheets tangled around her legs and she moved to get comfortable. The scent of Zach and of their lovemaking still lingered. It had been so different from what she'd expected, no shy fumbling, no embarrassment at not knowing what to do. Her hands had touched him, her mouth had responded to his. He had brought all the knowledge needed. And she had held her own. He had never suspected until that last moment. Slowly Caitlin drifted to sleep vaguely plagued by the thought that something was missing.

Zach slammed the truck into gear and pulled away from the old house, his temper barely in check. The streets were dark and empty. He pressed the accelerator and tore through town, heading for the Lazy H. Damn, he got just want he wanted. She'd been right, he'd decided to make a play for Caitlin the moment he spotted her in the bar. How the hell was he supposed to know she was a virgin? She'd flirted like the best of them. Made no protest about being picked up. She'd deliberately led him on.

His grip tightened on the steering wheel as his mind involuntarily relived the last couple of hours. There had been nothing to give him a clue. Her hands had been all over him. Her mouth gave new meaning to the art of kissing. She had held nothing back. How could any man be expected to know she'd been innocent?

From her eyes.

The thought shook him. He remembered thinking it was an act. But it hadn't been. She was innocent as a newborn babe, or had been. Damn! He pounded the wheel with one hand. For a moment he felt something close to shame. He should have left her alone when Joan told him to. He should have taken her home and dropped her at her door, telling her good-night. He sure as hell should not have moved so fast in bed. A virgin needed more time to get ready, needed to be calmed, soothed, gentled before the final act. But he'd been as randy as a teenager, unable to wait while her hands had danced across his skin, igniting him. Her mouth against his chest had about driven him crazy with wanting.

"It was nice."

Nice! He screeched around a curve, gripping the wheel, holding the truck on the road. Double damn, he had never had a woman tell him he had been *nice* in bed! Seething, he tried to rationalize the evening. He had a reason to be upset—she'd been a virgin. He'd never made love to one before. Even his fiancée had experimented in high school, long before he asked her to marry him. They'd been circumspect—until she'd been seduced by his brother.

After that betrayal, Zach felt everyone was fair game.

But he'd never been a woman's first.

For a moment he wondered what it would be like to be the only man a woman knew. To teach her every aspect of love, all the different ways it could be expressed, all the ways to please him. To know no one else had ever touched her. Would she stay satisfied? Or would she look for more, want other experiences to compare. If so, would he come in favorably?

Nice.

Probably not.

Hadn't Alissa turned to his brother while he himself had been stationed in Germany? Of course he had no doubt that while Sam probably had pulled out all the plugs, the ultimate decision had been hers. And she'd ignored the fact she was engaged when she'd accepted his brother's invitation. But she'd known by then that Sam was the one to inherit the ranch.

Black anger flared. Zach rolled down the window, the cool night air shocking him. He needed concentration to drive—not the old, furious thoughts about his fiancée and his brother. Betrayed by two people he should have been able to trust cut him deeply. He would never forget. Nor forgive.

Focus on Caitlin Delany, he thought. Or not. He didn't plan to see her again. She would misconstrue any further attention and expect more than he was willing to give. Ever. Burned once was more than enough. Burned by family and love was more than a man should expect to take. Only a fool would set himself up for another fall.

He shook off his thoughts, refusing to give in to them. He would never give his brother the satisfaction of knowing how deep the wounds had cut. Since he'd discovered their perfidy, he'd worn a mask of disinterest. No one knew how hard it had been, how hard it still was at times, to pretend it all meant nothing.

That everything that had happened in the past four years meant nothing.

But that was the role he'd chosen, and he would stick to it.

The gate for the Lazy H loomed on the left. Scarcely slowing for the turn, Zach felt the rear of the truck shimmy and skid when he wrenched the wheel. Compensating, he had it straight in only a second. The road to the main house was over a mile, but his place was just up on the right. Far enough that he could not see the house of his childhood, the house his brother now occupied. Far enough to give him breathing room and the illusion sometimes that he was on his own, that he'd made something of his life after all the dreams had crashed.

He jerked the truck to a stop and headed inside. Entering, he ignored the lights, slammed the door and moved to his bedroom in the back of the house. Shucking his clothes, the scent of Caitlin suddenly filled his nostrils. For a moment he closed his eyes, remembering. She'd been soft, warm, hungry. Her taste had been so sweet. Rubbing his hands over his face he shook his head, trying to dislodge the memories. She was just a woman. He'd had a lot since losing Alissa. Nothing special about this one. Just another in a long line.

Yet her image kept reappearing. Why? Usually he came home and went straight to sleep. He made it a practice to never stay the night at a woman's house. It might give rise to hopes he made sure they didn't have. He would let no one close again. That way, he'd avoid disappointment and heartache. It made for a lonely life, but what the hell, it was the only one he had, and he could live it as he wanted. And what he wanted was to be left alone. No ties, no commitments. Especially with a woman.

"It was nice."

The words rankled. Maybe he needed to show her *nice* wasn't the word to describe it. Maybe one more night would show her Zach Haller wasn't nice. That making love with him was exciting, hot, dangerous—but not *nice!*

Zach woke early Saturday morning. No matter how late he stayed out, he always woke before six. Taking a quick shower, he noted he didn't have his normal hangover. Maybe chasing after virgins wasn't totally bad. At least he felt halfway decent today. But the thought immediately brought images of Caitlin. Was she all right? Maybe he should check on her today and make sure—

Make sure what? She'd been pretty clear last night she had no expectations from him. She'd practically thrown him out.

Which suited him to a T. He wouldn't have stayed all night, anyway. But it rankled that she'd asked him to leave.

Dressed, Zach headed for the barn. He'd ride fences today. Not that he needed to, but being on a horse alone on the open range appealed to him. It was nothing like taking a jet through its paces, though, nothing like screaming across the desert basin at Mach One, the sky the limit. He frowned. It was gone, give it up.

"Hey, bro, up early after a night on the town, aren't you?" Sam sauntered into the barn as Zach finished saddling his horse.

Zach glanced at his brother, back to the horse. "Up early every day, just like you. What's your point?" They had achieved a certain civility between them, but Zach was hard-pressed to manage that most days.

"Thought you'd lie in bed with a hangover like your other weekends." Sam's tone mocked.

Zach ignored him, pulling the cinch tightly. Slapping the stirrup down, he gathered the reins.

"Heading out?" Sam asked, standing in the center of the barn. He didn't block the way, there was ample room on either side. But he acted as if he wanted to.

"Thought I'd check the fencing along the Marlstone's boundary. No one's checked that in a while," Zach replied neutrally.

"We'd have heard if any of our stock crossed onto their property. Marlstone gets fanatical about that. His men check all the time."

"No sense not doing our share," Zach returned as he started toward his brother. Would he have to push him aside, or step around? Anger shimmered near the surface as it did every time Zach came near Sam. Anger for the betrayal by his brother as well as for the actions of their father. He'd lived with it for four years. Would it cause him to explode one day?

"I have a new bull being delivered this afternoon. Be home by two so you can help get him in the pen. Thought I'd keep him near the house for a week or so before turning him loose on the range."

Zach stopped inches from Sam, staring him in the eye. The brothers were of similar coloring. Sam was heavier and a bit taller. When their father had died and left Sam in charge, Sam began cutting back on doing the actual ranch work. He was the big boss, giving orders to others and reveling in the position.

"This is my day off, and I can do what I want. Get your own damn bull situated. I'll be home when I feel like it," Zach said, his eyes narrowing. He was itching for a fight. Maybe this time Sam would oblige him.

"Talk like that can get you fired," Sam said, his eyes narrowing.

"Yeah? You couldn't run this place without me and you know it. But if you want to try it, let me know. I can light out and find another spread."

Sam stepped aside without a word, his tightened features the only acknowledgment he'd heard Zach's threat. He watched as Zach led his horse into the sunshine, mounted and rode away.

Zach smiled grimly. Maybe he should leave, let Sam run the place. It would go downhill fast enough to bankrupt him in a couple of years.

But the ranch belonged in small part to Zach as well, and was all he had left after his aborted career with the Air Force. He needed it for stability, for a tie to the past. But he still felt the sharp drop in his belly at the thought of his father leaving the major ownership portion to Sam. Would it have mattered as much if he still had his commission? Would he have cared as much then?

He'd already been home when his father died. The old man had never forgiven him for choosing the Air Force over the ranch, and had made sure his son knew it. He'd been obvious, leaving the majority to his older son and infant grandson.

Zach hoped he wasn't as obvious. He worked hard to show he didn't care about the ranch or women or much of anything. The mask had been in place so long now, he didn't even have to work constantly to keep it up.

One-night stands, moving to the next woman. Had Caitlin realized that was the plan? Or did she somehow think he'd come round again? Time she learned life's tough lessons. Nothing went the way a person planned. She'd probably find another man tonight and with one experience behind her, try again.

For some reason the idea disturbed him.

Kicking the horse, Zach tried to outride his thoughts.

Caitlin puttered around her apartment all day. She ironed the clothes she planned to wear to school, vacuumed each room and made sure she had enough food to last the week. She planned to concentrate on her new class for a few days, and wanted all the other chores of life out of the way.

As she worked, thoughts from last night crowded her mind. Even by morning's light, she'd still felt a lingering pleasure and that curious sense of incompleteness.

Pushing those feelings aside, she considered the man who whetted her curiosity. She wished she knew more about him. He intrigued her, fascinated her. If she went to the cowboy bar tonight, would he again seek her out? Or would she have to watch him make up to some other woman as Anita had had to do last night?

A pang hit her. Joan had clearly told her he was bad news. She should have listened. But was that part of his appeal—the wild man who was such a contrast to the people she'd known in Maryland? The heady feeling that such a man had singled her out for one night didn't fade.

She'd come to Texas to start her life. To find out what she'd been missing, to make some changes and live, for a change. She'd done that in spades last night. But she hoped there was more to life than that. Was there a happy balance?

When the phone rang, Caitlin flew across the room, hoping against hope that it would be Zach. She tried not to let her disappointment show when she recognized Joan's voice.

"Are you all right?" Joan demanded.

"Why wouldn't I be?" Caitlin sat on the edge of the chair. She refused to give status reports to her parents through Joan.

"I looked for you at one point last night and you were gone. Trevor told me Zach took you home. Did he try anything?"

Try? No, he succeeded!

"What I do with my life is my own affair." Caitlin cringed at the word. "I'm fine, Zach did not stay. You can report back to my parents and then leave me alone."

"Caitlin, I'm sorry. I won't call them. You have a right to live your life as you want. Please don't shut me out. We've been friends for a long time. You helped me out when I felt so lost at college, so far from home. I want to be a friend in return. What you do is your business. I'm not reporting in to your mother."

Caitlin took a deep breath. She and Joan had met as college freshmen six years ago. Yet she wondered if she could ever trust that friendship again. She felt betrayed and hurt. But she had a choice—make a clean break or retain a modicum of their former friendship. Grateful to Joan for her job and apartment, Caitlin elected to see what happened between them.

"I'm all set for school on Monday. Looking forward to it." Teaching a class of first graders would take her mind off Zach Haller, if nothing else, she thought.

They arranged to meet for lunch the first day, and Joan hung up. Caitlin slowly replaced the receiver. She knew Zach would not call, why had she hoped he would? And if he did? What would she find to say to him? The heat that had flowed in her veins had cooled. The rebellion that had sparked her actions had eased. She had nothing else to prove, except that she could make a life on her own.

Gazing off into the distance, she focused slowly on the room. The sunshine made the place sparkle. Pride began to grow. She'd made a start in changing her life. Two weeks ago she had been in Annapolis. Since discovering the truth, she'd driven all the way to Texas by herself, found an apartment, bought some furniture and accepted a job. And last night she'd become a woman.

The smile that lit her face couldn't be stopped. Giddy with excitement, she jumped up and twirled around the spacious room. Life was looking up! She was on her own and going to make her life anything she wanted. She'd stop being shy, stop being cautious and explore every avenue that presented itself. Time she became an adult, not her parents' little girl.

By the time she arrived at the cowboy bar at eight that night, Caitlin was a nervous wreck. She had dressed with care in her jeans and boots. Brushed her hair until it glowed. Her makeup was light, highlighting her blue eyes, since someone had once said they were her best feature. Excitement and anticipation had built all day. She was on her own tonight—no Joan. But she had met a few people last night. And she didn't have to stay if she didn't want to.

If she ran into Zach, she'd treat him coolly. She would

not throw herself at him. But if he asked her to dance, she'd accept. Nothing more. She had tried hard all day to put their lovemaking in perspective. It had been a good introduction to passion, but she wanted more. And she finally decided the missing ingredient had been genuine caring. Affection for the other person would be important, she thought. And it had been missing when two almost strangers made love.

She'd grown up a bit as a result of last night, however. Tonight she planned to play it cool. Be friendly to other cowboys. Let Zach see that she was not the romantic innocent he called her, that she had no designs on him.

The music was as loud as last night, the smoke thick and hazy. Caitlin smiled as she stepped inside. It felt like coming home as her gaze traveled around the room. When she saw Lindsay Marquette, the substitute teacher she'd met on Thursday, she waved at her and headed for the table, almost bumping into a waitress with a tray of beer when she caught sight of Zach Haller at a pool table. He leaned over for a shot, his concentration on the ball.

Her heart began to pump hard against her chest. Her palms grew damp. He was already here and not dancing. Could he have been waiting for her to arrive?

Lindsay yanked an empty chair over to the already crowded table. When Caitlin sat down, Lindsay made quick work of introducing her to the rest of the group. Smiling, Caitlin tried to keep all the names straight, tried to pay attention to the conversation that flowed. Conscious of Zach Haller only a few yards away, however, her concentration was split. Would he even speak to her tonight?

"There you are, you bastard!" An irate woman's voice rose above the din and silenced part of the room.

Caitlin spun around. Standing in the doorway was a tall, buxom, red-haired woman. Fire almost shot from her eyes as she glared at Zach. Caitlin watched as Zach slowly stood, turned around and leaned against the pool table.

"Looking for me, darlin'?" he drawled.

"You better believe it!" The furious woman took a step closer, her hands fisted at her side, her voice loud and clear. "I'm pregnant and just who do you think the daddy is?"

Four

Caitlin froze, her eyes swiveling to Zach. Blood pounded in her veins. For one awful moment she imagined herself in the same situation—if Zach hadn't insisted on using protection last night. She'd been so far gone in passion she hadn't had two thoughts that made sense. But Zach had seen to it. Had he learned from an earlier mistake? Somehow she'd thought it an innate trait—his caution. Anyone who could stop cold and take the time to make sure they had protection wasn't likely to forget at another time. Was he?

And his comment about a child being loved into existence echoed in her mind.

Studying him, she noticed the signs of strain around his mouth. But a heartbeat later, she wondered if she'd imagined them.

He smiled, took a sip from the long-neck beer and shook his head at the angry woman stomping over to him. Fleetingly his hard gaze scanned the room. Seeing the watchful eyes of everyone present seemed to strengthen him. He stood taller, as if in defiance. Alone he faced the fury as everyone in the room watched.

"Not me, babe," he drawled.

Margot Simmons stopped inches in front of him, glaring up at him, her rage almost a palpable thing. "Yes, you…you arrogant bastard! You're the only one I've slept with since Bobby and I broke up last August. At Tilly's party before Thanksgiving, remember? I'm not having this kid alone, cowboy, I can guaran-damn-tee you that!"

"It's not mine, babe," he said again.

Gradually the level of conversation rose, as people turned away from the scene by the pool table to discuss what was happening. Lindsay nudged Caitlin.

"Not one of our shining stars, I'm afraid," she said. "I'm not surprised his reckless ways have caught up with him."

"What?" Loath to turn away, Caitlin was even more fearful of speculation if she paid too much attention. How many people here remembered she'd left with Zach last night? Not knowing what to think, she longed for the peace of her apartment. She'd been foolish last night. Only by the grace of God—no that wasn't right. Zach had been very adamant about making sure they had birth control. He had been as involved in the moment as she, yet he'd stopped to make sure it was taken care of. Would he have ignored that last November? She had to admit she didn't know the man very well. But a glimmer of doubt surfaced.

"Zach Haller's our local bad boy," Lindsay said almost proudly.

Caitlin didn't like Lindsay's attitude. She seemed almost gleeful with the turn of events. It seemed a shame to Caitlin. If he'd gotten the woman pregnant, he'd have to marry her. And after last night she knew he didn't want to be tied down. Footloose and fancy-free—that summed up that cowboy. Instead of feeling sorry for him, however, Lindsay seemed to revel in the situation. Why?

Joan didn't seem to like him, either. She'd alluded to some huge scandal. While Joan had refused to discuss it, Caitlin knew Lindsay wouldn't have the same reticence. She'd bet a beer Lindsay would delight in dishing up gossip. The question was, did she want to hear it? And did she want to hang around a woman who loved to gossip? She had her own reputation to guard.

"What's he done that's so bad?" Caitlin asked, hoping she sounded casual.

"Now, obviously, getting a woman pregnant and then denying it. Just like the man, trying to slip out from his responsibilities. He was always in trouble as a teenager—with his father and the law."

"With the law?"

"You know, soaping windows, graffiti, herding cattle down main street and snarling traffic—things like that. Nothing major, just enough to annoy everyone. Get the deputies out to his father's place more than once."

Caitlin thought of the small main road through town. It wouldn't take much to snarl traffic—but then there wasn't much traffic, either. Nothing like a real city. That was the extent of his crimes? Youthful high jinks?

"Give him a break," one of the men at the table interrupted. Caitlin couldn't remember his name, was it Steve or was he Paul? "He earned his way into the Air Force Academy, that's no small feat in itself. And it sure wasn't his fault his brother stole his fiancée, or that his plane crashed. Any guy would cut loose a bit after a string of bad luck like that."

"Sure, stand up for the man. You guys close rank."

"He said he wasn't the father," Caitlin said. Was she defending the man? She hardly knew him. Color stained her cheeks as she remembered the two of them together last night. She'd come to know his body quite well. But it wasn't the same thing as knowing the *man*.

"Like we can believe anything he says."

"Care to dance?" The lanky cowboy from last night stood near the table, smiling down at Caitlin.

"Sure thing," Caitlin replied with alacrity. Was his name Vic? She wished she could remember. The dance would help her escape the malicious maligning of a man's name. And maybe to escape her own thoughts. As they wound their way through the tables to the dance floor, Caitlin caught a glimpse of Zach and Margot huddled close together. They seemed to be arguing. At least they kept their voices down—not sharing everything with the entire town. But Caitlin wished she could hear what they said, wished she knew if Zach would lie about something like that, or if he was telling the truth. If so, did that make Margot the liar?

Before the dance ended, Caitlin knew she wasn't going to find the same excitement tonight as she had the previous one. Maybe because she was tired. Or maybe the novelty had begun to wear off. This was not her first night in a cowboy bar. Had the thrill of being on her own ended so quickly?

Despite constant admonishments to herself, she found she was aware of Zach and Margot every moment. She longed to hear what they discussed, wished she could get some reassurance from Zach that he was not that baby's father, that he didn't sleep with a different woman every night. Something to show that last night had been special and not some tawdry little one-night stand.

It had been special for her—though not as complete or wondrous as she'd always imagined. Could it be that sex was overrated?

Caitlin almost stumbled when she saw Zach rise and put his arm around the woman's shoulder. He looked up and met her gaze, their eyes locking for several seconds. Then he responded to something Margot said, and in only seconds, they left the bar.

And with his going, Caitlin lost the last bit of interest in remaining.

She danced with several other men, had a beer with her new colleagues and then pleaded tiredness.

"But you haven't been here that long," Lindsay protested when Caitlin began to say good-night.

"I was up late last night and want to be well rested for Monday. I enjoyed meeting everyone," Caitlin said, hoping again no one would speculate on why she'd been up late last night. She wanted to leave with her reputation intact.

Despite the conversation that had sprung up after Margot's dramatic accusation, the recounting of several of Zach's more notorious escapades, Caitlin had a niggling feeling something wasn't right. As she started her car, she remembered last night. Zach had had only one beer the entire evening. He'd not been the slightest bit intoxicated as the reports had indicated was his habit. And he'd been so very cautious about birth control. Somehow she didn't see him as the philandering type. No matter what his reputation indicated. And especially not as someone who would get a woman pregnant and then not step up to his responsibilities.

Which apparently made her out as a colossal fool, a naive woman who still had starry-eyed optimism and fairy-tale heroes in mind. She should be extremely grateful her name had not been linked with his. As a new schoolteacher, she needed to keep her reputation spotless. She couldn't jeopardize her position. Even before Margot's startling announcement, Caitlin had known there was no long-term relationship possible between her and that sexy cowboy. Tonight just confirmed it.

But it didn't explain why she felt so let down after he left. It wasn't as if she wanted a repeat of the previous night. Though one dance would have been nice.

* * *

Zach hit his palm against the steering wheel and let loose a string of curses. What was one more blow of bad luck with the way his life was going? Why didn't he just accept nothing would go right ever again and get on with it? He pushed open the door of the canted truck and went to the front to access the damage. Swerving to avoid that dog had been a damn-fool stunt. How many times had he been told to keep on driving, a person's life was worth more than an animal's. But no, he had to swerve to avoid the blasted mutt and ended up in a ditch.

The truck's right fender lay crumpled against the opposite side of the drainage culvert. The right tire was flat, the wheel rim bent a little.

"I'll be lucky if I didn't bust the axle," he muttered, stooping down and trying to determine the extent of damage in the dark. He'd driven a distraught Margot home and spent some time trying to calm her down. She stuck to her story that he was the father despite his repeated denials. Hell, if she thought to stick him with her kid, she'd better come up with a better story that she had. He'd deny it to kingdom come. Once the baby was old enough he'd demand DNA testing to prove it. He had never slept with the woman, how could she accuse him?

Of course the entire town would believe her. It was easier than accusing someone else, and Margot knew it. But why had she picked on him?

Slowly he straightened. He couldn't get the truck out tonight. It would take a tow truck, and he knew Jerry Achison didn't like going out to wrecks that could wait until morning. Besides, the last thing he wanted was a run-in with Sheriff Marton. One beer didn't make a man drunk, but the sheriff would still make a big deal out of breath analysis and keep him overnight. He didn't need the hassle.

Straightening, he looked up and down the road. He'd be home by now if he hadn't taken Margot home. This stretch of highway didn't have any houses on it, but it wasn't far to one of the side roads that did. He could call—

Zach sighed. He didn't want to call anyone.

Leaning against the side of the pickup, he crossed his arms and weighed the different options. Glancing up, arrested by the display of twinkling stars in the inky blackness of the night sky, he was transported back to the days he could fly. Night flights when the stars were so crystal clear he felt as if he could scoop up a handful just by reaching out. Tonight reminded him of that. It was beautiful.

The burning ache began. He'd never fly jets at Mach One again. He'd be lucky to pass any flying test now. The accident had seen to that. At the time he'd been grateful he'd lived. Now he wasn't so sure it had been such a great thing. He couldn't fly, had no wife, had no reputation to speak of, and fought with his brother endlessly over the management of the ranch. Why?

He ought to just pack up and head for parts unknown. What stubbornness kept him in Tumbleweed? Granted, he had a few friends, but every one of them would believe Margot. His behavior over these past few years would see to that. But better their scorn than their pity. The last thing he wanted was anyone to feel sorry for him.

A car sounded in the distance, its lights growing closer by the second. Idly Zach watched as it approached and slowed, stopping just a few feet beyond him. Maryland plates. Zach smiled cynically. Would the new schoolteacher do her good deed tonight and offer him a place to stay? After kicking him out last night, he highly doubted it.

Pushing away from the truck, he walked down the highway until he reached the driver's door. Caitlin had rolled down her window.

"What happened?" she asked.

"Dodged a dog, ended up in the ditch."

"Can't you get the truck out?"

"Not without a tow. You got anything in your car that could pull me out?"

She shook her head. "Want a ride to a service station?" she asked.

"None open now. It'll have to wait until morning." He stooped until his face was level with the opening. She was hard to see in the dark, but he could smell her sweet scent and hear her soft Southern voice. And every second he grew more aware of what they'd shared last night.

He wanted her again.

And knew he hadn't a snowball's chance in hell.

"What are you going to do? You can't stay here all night," she said.

"Someone will be along soon."

"I'm along now. Get in, I'll give you a ride home."

"Nah, it's too far out."

"Too far out of what?"

"Too far out of your way," he said, wishing he could see her blue eyes again, see the hint of color flush and fade in her cheeks.

"You gave me a ride last night, I can give you one tonight," she said reasonably.

Zach almost groaned, remembering the ride they'd shared last night. Desire tightened its grip. She hadn't a clue what she was doing to him. And probably wouldn't care. In fact, he was surprised she would even risk it. She'd been at the bar tonight when Margot had made her accusation. He'd seen the shocked expression on Caitlin's face. How brave of her to stop.

"Come on and get in," Caitlin repeated.

He rose and went around the back of the car with one last glance at his truck. He'd probably be safer staying the night in it. But he couldn't resist a few minutes with Caitlin.

"You have to give the directions," she said when he was seated.

"About a mile up the road there's a junction with Route 92, turn left and head out about five miles."

He leaned against the seat and turned slightly so he could watch her. The faint illumination from the dashboard silhouetted her features, her cute nose and the flawless beauty of her skin. He took a breath and instantly regretted it as her scent filled him. He wanted to reach over and pull her into his arms, bury his nose against her neck and drink in her unique fragrance. He remembered her taste, and his mouth yearned for another sample. Her mouth had been honey-sweet, as had her neck, her nipples. As the memory filled him, it became blatantly obvious that his body wanted her more tonight than last night. Shifting on the seat, he tried to ease the growing tightness in his jeans. At the rate he was going, he wouldn't be able to walk when they reached home!

"You left early," he commented. He had to do something or go crazy.

"So did you," she returned.

"I took Margot home."

"She's the one gunning for you, I believe Anita said," Caitlin responded primly.

Zach chuckled, though he found nothing funny about the situation. "I'm not the daddy of her baby."

"So you said."

"So I mean!" Anger spiced his tone. Taking a deep breath, Zach calmed himself. No sense getting riled every time someone doubted him—he'd never have a moment's peace.

"Okay," Caitlin said easily.

"Okay?"

"Well, one of you should know. But I did wonder where birth control came into it. I mean last night you were so adamant. Was that a recent conversion? Or have you always been so conscientious?"

"I've been careful since I first started seeing women."

She smiled and threw him a glance. "Seeing women? How quaint."

"I can be crude, if you wish."

She shook her head. "So what's the story, why is she accusing you if you aren't the father?"

"I don't know. I can't decide if she really thinks it is me," he said, "or if she's out to get someone to support her and I look like the likely bet." He leaned back and gaze out at the highway. Margot seemed to believe he was the one she'd slept with in November, or she was a damned fine actress. But he knew he hadn't. They'd been drinking heavily at the party, danced together a few times, kissed a bit. But he'd remember if he'd gone to bed with her.

As far as he could recall, he'd left to go home around midnight. He didn't remember much about the drive and was just thankful he hadn't crashed into someone. The hangover the next morning was enough to make him swear off drinking altogether. Almost.

"But if you know it wasn't you, then who? Does someone in town look like you? Could she have mistaken him for you?" Caitlin asked.

Zach sucked in a breath. *Sam looked like him.* Or rather he looked like his older brother. Not enough to be twins, but close enough no one doubted they were brothers. Could Sam have been the one? Had Margot really gotten them mixed up, or were the two of them trying some kind of con game? He wouldn't put it past his brother. But would Margot try something like that?

"Zach?"

"What? Watch up on your left, there'll be fencing and then a gate. Turn in and drive up about a mile." He'd have to give this some thought. Sam had one son. Was he going to be expecting his second child? If Sam thought he could railroad him into accepting his kid as his own, Zach would set him straight pronto. It was bad enough knowing that if Alissa had married him, he'd be the one with a son now instead of Sam. But he was not going to take on the responsibility of another man's child.

Suddenly a thought struck Zach. Sam was petitioning the courts to get joint custody of his boy, to share with Alissa. While Sam was a single man right now, Zach suspected the courts wouldn't look too favorably on his getting custody if he was the type to get another woman pregnant and refuse to marry her. As far as Zach knew, Sam didn't even like Margot Simmons. So did it make sense he'd have slept with her?

Damn, he wished he could remember more about that party. But it had just been one of many he'd gone to over the years, nothing special. Just a means to fill an evening, to try to forget.

"So?" Caitlin prodded.

"So what? The house will be up on the right in a minute."

"Okay. I mean, is there someone else in town that Margot might have gotten you confused with?"

"No."

"I'd think it hard for a woman to imagine someone else, when she was making love with a man," she said thoughtfully.

"Drop it, Caitlin. It doesn't matter. The kid isn't mine, and I'm not going to take responsibility for something I didn't do. I have enough on my plate as it is."

Caitlin slowed as they approached his house. It wasn't much more than a cabin. Zach wondered what she'd think of it when she saw it. Especially if she ever compared it to the main house.

"This it?"

"Yes. Just pull in front, you'll have room to turn around."

Stopping the car, she turned to look at him but didn't say a word.

What could she say, he wondered cynically. *Glad it was*

Margot, not me that you got pregnant? Damn. He opened the door.

"Thanks, I owe you."

"I don't think so," she said softly. "Zach, maybe you should—"

He leaned back in, studying her in the faint dome light. "Don't worry about me, Schoolteacher. I always land on my feet, haven't you heard?"

He wanted to drag her across the seat, kiss her silly and take her straight to bed. But he knew the futility of that thought. She was not for him. No woman was. That had been hammered home enough. And even Margot's trying to trap him only convinced him of the perfidy of the gender. "Drive home now, Caitlin. Forget we ever met."

He closed the car door and turned away, one of the hardest things he'd ever done in a life full of hard choices. But he knew she wasn't for him. And the sooner he put her out of his mind, the better.

Caitlin watched him stride into the house and close the door. Slowly she turned her car around and headed back toward town. Something was wrong, but she didn't know enough to speculate what it was—aside from her own riotous senses around a man who definitely wasn't interested. Swallowing hard, she concentrated on driving and tried to ignore the clamoring of her body. She would not have objected to a kiss.

"Right, and another toss in the hay, no doubt," she said scathingly. Hadn't last night taught her anything? And if it hadn't, tonight's scenario should have. But something still bothered her about that. Zach said he hadn't slept with Margot. Did she understand enough about human nature to know when someone was lying? She thought he was telling the truth, but what if he was just a smooth operator, dashing from one woman to another and never taking responsibility? She had her own instinct to guide her, but nothing else.

But that instinct insisted he would own up to his responsibilities. Yet he'd sure responded quickly with a denial when she asked if Margot could have confused him with someone else. Too quickly?

Not that any of it mattered. She had had a one-night stand, a fling. Now she would settle down and become a proper citizen of Tumbleweed. And if it meant staying away from Zach, there should be no problem. It wasn't as if they had anything going between them.

Except the sizzling memory of one night in bed.

It seemed to Caitlin that the primary topic of conversation when she started work at Tumbleweed Elementary School centered around Zach Haller. The best secret is one everyone already knows. People made references to his having been a rebellious teenager, and then comments about his father. Because everyone except her knew his background, they never explained. And she dare not inquire. She was trying to ignore the feelings that shimmered whenever she thought about him. He was totally out of her realm. Joan had been right, he was not for her.

But curiosity raged about his accident, about his fiancée and his brother. There were tantalizing hints and innuendoes dropped until she thought she would scream if she didn't find out exactly what every one meant.

Despite the talk, she remembered him differently from what the gossip made him out to be. He'd swept her off her feet, made her feel exciting—all woman. The first and only man to do so. Would there always be a soft spot in her heart for him because of that? And because of their one night together?

Daydreams were hard to come by when teaching a class of rambunctious first-graders, yet at the oddest moments, Zach would pop into mind.

Sharing lunch the first day with Joan, Caitlin found herself wishing they could regain their earlier ease. But she felt too cautious. Maybe after being on her own for a while, she would learn to trust her friends. Until then she would guard everything she said just in case Joan was still in touch with her mother.

Teaching had been her goal, and now she had achieved it. She delighted in the wide-eyed wonder of her students. Quiet satisfaction filled her as she thought ahead to the rest of the school year.

Wednesday after school, Caitlin headed into town. She had pictures to hang and needed nails and hangers. Locating the hardware store, adjacent to the feed store, she began to wander up and down the aisles, looking for the items she needed. She'd have to buy a hammer. When she found the display, she studied each one. The larger ones, obviously, were more than she needed. But there must have been at least a dozen different kinds. She just wanted something to bang in a few nails.

Reaching up to take one down, she practiced swinging it.

"Taking up a new profession?" a familiar voice drawled behind her.

Turning, she almost bumped into Zach.

"No." She tested the weight of the hammer. "I want to hang some pictures and don't have the necessary tools. Do you think this hammer will do for me?"

He reached out and took it from her hand, brushing his fingers across hers. Caitlin almost dropped the tool. Tingling currents shot up her arm, and her entire body grew warm. She could remember those hands on her last Friday night, the roughened calluses igniting her skin in a heated conflagration that still left her breathless whenever she remembered. Which she did frequently and at the most embarrassing times. Would the memory of that night gradually fade? Or was she destined to relive it in her mind over and over until she could repeat it?

"Good balance. Nice all-around hammer. More than you

need for a few pictures hooks, but would be of use for other projects you might have.''

"Like what?'' She couldn't think of anything except how close he stood, how tired he looked, how his hat rode low on his forehead and how much she wanted to touch him. Just brush her fingers along his jaw or trace her fingertips along his chest. To feel that remembered heat, the strength of his muscles.

Clenching her fists, she glared at the hammer. She had to buy her supplies and leave, not lust after some wild cowboy. Instantly the memory of Saturday night imposed itself. What had happened with Margot?

"Repairs, building projects. I don't know, what do you think?''

She thought she'd go crazy if she didn't get out of the store soon.

"Okay, thanks.'' She reached out to take the hammer, her hand covering his. She had her wish, only now that she was touching him, she didn't want to stop.

The forefinger of his free hand came beneath her chin and tilted her head. Wide-eyed, Caitlin stared up into his dark blue eyes. A foreign hunger built. She wanted him. Had she become a sex addict after one night with a man?

"You need a tape measurer, and a level wouldn't hurt. Did you get the hooks?''

She shook her head, mesmerized by his gaze. She could lose herself in this man. And that way lay danger. He didn't want any long-term affair. Not that she did. Spreading her wings and testing herself didn't mean limiting herself to one man. Swallowing hard, she stepped back, tugging the hammer from his grasp.

"I haven't finished shopping.''

"I could help you find the things. I'm familiar with the store.''

It made sense. She nodded. "Thanks. This is the first

time I've been in a hardware store. It's a bit overwhelming."

Zach made short work of locating the items she needed, carrying them easily in one hand: tape measure, small level, picture hooks. He walked with her to the cash register.

"Want me to give you a hand with these?" he asked as they waited behind the only other customer.

"With hanging the pictures?" she asked. Was the offer genuine, or did he have something else in mind? She glanced at him. His steady gaze gave nothing away as he nodded. She'd be a fool to turn down an offer like that. She hadn't a clue how to hang pictures. If he could teach her, she'd have the skill for life.

"That'd be great. Do you have time? Did you come here to shop?"

"To order some more hardware for fencing. I placed the order and was on my way out when I spotted you. I have enough time to stop by to hang a few pictures...if you want to take that chance that's all I'll do."

"What else?" she asked unsure if he was teasing her or serious.

He leaned close; his hat brushed her head as his gaze dropped to her mouth. "Maybe try to change that impression you had of last Friday night," he said in a low voice.

Caitlin blushed to the roots of her hair. Glancing around hastily, she glared at him. "Hush, someone will hear you."

"And if they do?"

"Aren't you in enough trouble with Margot without giving everyone the impression you—"

He tapped her chin. "Margot doesn't concern you. I told you I'm not the father of her baby."

"Did you think of anyone else in town who might be?"

"Are you two going to jaw all day, or buy those things in your hands?" a gruff voice said.

Caitlin turned and stepped up to the counter. She placed the hammer down and drew her wallet from her purse as

Zach deposited the items he'd carried. Feeling self-conscious at the suspicious look the proprietor gave first her then Zach, she tried to force a cool expression of disinterest.

"Don't spread yourself too thin, boy," the man admonished Zach.

Caitlin remained silent, taking her change. Zach picked up the bag and urged her out of the store.

"Damn, I'll be thirty my next birthday. I'm no boy."

She wondered if she'd ever understand men. Here Zach was, rumored to be a troublemaker of the first order, up to his neck in accusations of paternity, and he was upset because some old man called him a boy.

Five

***

Caitlin had about ten minutes to reconsider her actions. That was the duration of the drive from the hardware store to her apartment. Was she being a total idiot to let the man claim even part of her time? Tilting her chin, she strengthened her resolve. Second-guessing everything was her mother's trait. She was breaking loose and living life on her terms. And she would not have any regrets. Zach had done nothing to warrant her suspicions—at least, not directly with her.

It was just to hang a few pictures, she told herself as she parked her car. Taking a breath, she tried to push from her mind the memories of the last time Zach had been in her apartment. She needed to concentrate on the task at hand, focus on the present, not remember something best forgotten.

He waited on the porch, leaning casually against the post, his arms crossed as he watched her walk toward him— looking rugged and masculine. Caitlin swallowed hard, her heart fluttering madly in her chest. Had this been a mistake? She had no business tempting fate, and her own resolve, by inviting him into her house again. Yet she didn't have a polite way to refuse at this point. And she could use the help.

"Change your mind?" Zach asked as she stepped up on the porch with him.

"What do you mean?" Did the man read minds? Or had her expression given away her thoughts?

He leaned close, his fingers brushing against her hair. Caitlin's every nerve ending stood at attention. Holding her breath, she waited for the next move in this dangerous escapade. Yearned for more. Slowly Zach leaned forward until his breath brushed against her cheeks.

"Change your mind about asking the big bad cowboy into your house. Who knows what might happen?"

"I can guess," she said with some asperity. It was one thing to change her mind, something else to let him know. Or give any indication she wasn't up to his challenge. She was her own woman now. And it was time to act like it.

"Something to show you that I'm not nice," he confirmed.

Puzzled, she shook her head. "I don't get it."

"Last Friday just before I left, you told me it was nice."

She nodded—*nice* had not been the precise word she should have used. But glorious and exciting and erotic were beyond her capability to convey to a near stranger.

Narrowing his eyes, he came even closer, until Caitlin thought he'd kiss her again. Suddenly she realized she wanted him to. She was more knowledgeable about things since her introduction to passion, and she could respond this time. Let herself enjoy what he offered, knowing it was just another step on her road to emancipation.

"Dammit, no woman has ever said my lovemaking was nice! I'm not nice!" He spaced the words, stating each firmly, clearly.

Blinking, Caitlin watched him warily. "Is that an insult?"

"Damn straight it is."

"Oh." Men were so bizarre. "Should I have said it was awful?"

"I would have preferred something to show you recognized it was great sex."

Heat washed through her. It had been great, even though she felt it missed something. But that was not something she was comfortable saying. Breaking eye contact, she stepped hastily away. "If you want to help me put up my pictures, come in. If you stopped just to rehash last Friday, forget it."

Opening the door, she ran lightly up the steps, conscious of his heavy tread behind her. Her heart skipped a beat then pounded rapidly in her chest. She opened her door, hoping they could hang the pictures in record time so he'd leave. She hoped nothing would happen in the meantime. How strong was she?

Zach tossed his hat on the sofa as before, shrugged out of his jacket. "Which one first?" Hefting the bag, he looked at Caitlin.

"I have two I brought from home I want hung in the hallway. Then I bought these at that secondhand store off Main Street yesterday. I think they're colorful." She peeped up at him. What would he think of her choices?

He easily lifted the first picture, a romantic sea scene that had hung in her bedroom in Maryland for as long as she could remember. She loved it. But it was time to have something different in her bedroom now. The hall would suffice.

Zach wasted few motions locating the position for the painting, measuring the space and driving in the nail. Caitlin watched, fascinated. The next one, he motioned her over.

"You'll never learn if you don't try it," he said, handing

her the tape. Copying his actions, she measured, marked the wall, and wielded the hammer awkwardly.

"Like this." He moved behind her, his arm coming around her when his hand covered hers. Swinging her arm, he hit the nail squarely on its head.

Caitlin could scarcely breathe. His heat seemed to envelop her. His hard chest pressed against her back, his arm stretched out along hers. The wall blurred as she became caught up in the tingling sense of heightened awareness that washed through her. He was the only man to send such sparks through her. Was it the novelty of being alone with a man? Or was there something special about Zach?

She hadn't felt like this with the other cowboys she'd danced with at the bar last weekend. While she still felt a modicum of control, she stepped aside. "Thanks," she said breathlessly. "I'll try the next one on my own."

In only a few moments, every painting was in place. Despite her shaky start, Caitlin's sense of accomplishment threatened to spill out. Granted, others might have learned such skills as teenagers, hanging pictures and posters in their room. But better to learn late than never.

The huge picture over the faux mantel was her favorite— an oil painting of the Rockies. The sky almost hurt her eyes it was so blue. The granite of the peaks seemed three dimensional. Feeling as free as an eagle, she gazed at it in delight. Each picture added life and color to her rooms. Smiling in quiet satisfaction, she was pleased with her choices. In pictures, that is. Warily she glanced at Zach. Would he leave now?

"Thank you for helping me. It would have taken me forever," she said. "And I would have spent hours getting them straight."

Zach shrugged. "No problem."

Biting her lip, she turned to put the hammer in the closet. Would he try something now? And if he did, could she resist?

"Want some coffee or something before you leave?" Ever polite, just as her parents had taught her.

He threw a taunting smile in her direction. "Sure. I'm happy to stay."

"It won't take long. I know you probably have to get back to your own work."

Zach watched her hurry to the kitchen—so much for finesse. She couldn't wait to get rid of him. But he had no intention of leaving quite so soon. He'd done nothing but think about the pretty schoolteacher since he'd left her place last Friday night. Curious, he wanted to find out more about her. And maybe see if the sparks they had ignited could flare again.

He walked to the kitchen door and leaned against the jamb, watching her bustle around the small room. She looked bright and pretty as she reached up for the coffee. He glimpsed a sliver of pale skin beneath her blouse when she raised her arms. The impact was instantaneous. He wanted her. And not just to counter that accusation of being nice. He wanted her with a deep-seated desire that startled him.

Why Caitlin? For the novelty? Unlike the other women he knew, she had a freshness and innocence that tantalized and tormented. She'd been untouched the other night. Knowing he was the only man to have slept with her never left his thoughts. He wanted to do it again.

What would she do if he crossed the room and took her into his arms? Succumb to the temptation or slap his face and back away? He took a breath. There was only one way to find out.

She spun around when she heard his step, her eyes widening as he approached.

"It's not ready yet," she said.

"I am," he said, reaching out for her. Drawing her slowly into his embrace, he searched her eyes for a sign indicating how she felt. Confusion shone there. Yet when he lowered his face to hers, she tilted hers up to meet him. A good sign, he thought before his mouth covered hers.

She was soft and warm and tasted as he remembered—sweet and innocent. How could someone *taste* innocent? He didn't stop to analyze it, only went with the flow. Deepening the kiss, he pulled her snugly against him, reveling in the softness of her body, the press of her breasts, the sweet floral scent that seemed to invade every cell. After only a second, her arms encircled his neck and held on. Coherent thought fled as passion built.

Hot and sexy, Caitlin met his every need. His hands molded her body as he traced them over her back, from her shoulders to the soft curves of her hips. Lifting her slightly, he nestled against her, spreading his legs to better support them both.

The scent of her skin and the brewing coffee filled him. The taste of Caitlin overrode everything except his desire to strip the clothes from her and take her straight to bed. This time he'd stay. She wouldn't throw him out immediately, not if her response was anything to go by. Not as unsure as the first time, but still tentative, her hands moved against his shoulders, testing his strength, learning his body.

Except she was pushing against him. He wanted her to draw him closer.

She pulled back, pushing hard. "Stop, please."

"What?" Zach opened his eyes. She gazed up at him, her mouth rosy and slightly swollen, damp from his kisses. He licked her lip, trying to soothe. Maybe he'd been too hard.

"Stop, Zach. We can't do this."

"Why not?"

"It's not right."

"Why the hell not?" He let his arms drop, leaned against the counter, glaring at her. "It was all right on Friday night. Why not now?" Blood pounded through his veins, he wanted her and she pushed him away. Anger threatened. Was she playing some kind of game?

"I'm sorry, it's my fault," she said, clearing her throat. "I thought we said no strings."

"I'm not looking for strings," he muttered.

"Just another roll in the hay."

"So? It's not like we haven't done it before."

"I know. It's just—"

Color stained her cheeks. He'd wanted to see that pale pink sheen, but not if she was embarrassed. He didn't want her regretting their night together. He felt the thought hit like a kick.

"Just what?"

The coffee machine stopped. Caitlin turned and drew the carafe and poured two cups of coffee. Zach could see her hands trembling. At least she wasn't unaffected by their kiss. So why did she stop?

"We don't know each other very well, and I think anything else should wait until I know the person better," she said, pushing the cup near him, leaving it on the counter for him to pick up.

"How much better?" He didn't like the way the discussion was going. What if she didn't like him if she got to know him better? Hell, who was he trying to fool—he had no intentions of getting mixed up in getting to know each other. If she didn't want another tumble, he'd find someone who did.

Anita's image came to mind. He frowned. He was not interested in Anita Black. Nor Margot Simmons. Nor any other woman in town. He wanted Caitlin. Cautiously he studied her. Back off, he warned himself. He'd been burned once, and vowed to never repeat his mistake. Back off.

"I don't know, just better, or more, or something." She took her cup and headed for the living room.

Zach snatched up the coffee and took a long drink. It was hot, burned his mouth, but he didn't care. He'd like to pitch it against the pristine white wall of her neat little kitchen, stalk into the other room and—

And what? Join in some tea party discussion of their backgrounds, their likes and dislikes? He'd tried that once. Remembering the long discussions he and Alissa'd had getting to know each other. In the end it had proved nothing. He hadn't known her at all. Never suspected she would switch allegiance so quickly. Never caught on to the game until it was too late.

"Zach?"

With a sigh he pushed off and headed into the other room.

"I'm not much for exchanging life histories, Caitlin. I think I'll push off now."

"Wait, don't leave right away. Stay and visit for a little while."

"I told you I don't want some forever-after kind of affair."

"I don't either, at least not now. But we could maybe become friends. I've never had a man for a friend. In fact, I haven't had a lot of friends period."

"Why not?" He sat on the edge of one of her chairs and waited for her answer. She was a pretty woman, had a nice disposition, why hadn't she been inundated with boyfriends? She should have scads of girlfriends to share confidences with.

"It's tied up with my being here. I don't want to bore you. I'd rather hear about your stint in the Air Force. More than one person's mentioned you went to the Academy, on a full scholarship, no less. Your parents must have been proud of you!"

He shook his head. "Wrong on that one, Teacher. My old man was furious. He wanted both his sons to stay and run the ranch. What did I think he'd busted his butt for all those years—to see me go flying off with no sense of fam-

ily or responsibility?'' He smiled wryly, the old hurt long
ago numbed.

The shock of surprise showed clearly on her face. She
was so transparent. Did she have a clue?

''Is that why you came back to the ranch? To work on
it like your father wanted? I would have thought if you
went to the Academy, you must have wanted to make the
Air Force your life's work. What happened?''

The question caught him unaware. Suddenly the old ache
surfaced. The unfairness threatened to overwhelm him. So
much for numbness. Sheer effort kept his face expression-
less. It was over. Nothing was going to change by talking
about it. And pity was an emotion he would not tolerate—
from himself or anyone else!

''I was in a crash. Can't fly anymore so I opted out.''
Short, succinct.

''An airplane crash? Were you hurt? Of course you were,
you must have been. What happened?''

He didn't like talking about it, didn't like thinking about
it. Yet something about the concern clearly written on her
face relaxed his guard. Leaning back in the chair, he stuck
his legs out, one hand holding the coffee, the other tucked
into his pocket. He couldn't avoid it forever. It had happened. It was part of his life.

''I was stationed in Germany at the time, just flying a
routine training mission. Something went wrong with the
local radar control, and some small jet flew into our flight
path. I tried to avoid him, but he was a novice and scared
to death. Before I knew it, he plowed right into the back
of my aircraft, sheered off the tail. I bailed out before the
plane crashed. Tangled with some trees on landing. Suffered damage to the peripheral vision in my left eye. I was
grounded—can't fly anymore.'' Proud of the nonchalant
tone to his voice, Zach took another sip of coffee. Even his
hand was rock steady.

Sympathy filled her eyes. ''I'm sorry.''

"Yeah, well these things happen."

"I bet it felt devastating. You loved to fly, didn't you?" she asked softly.

He glanced at her, then away. Oh, yes, he'd loved to fly. It had been the only thing he'd wanted from the time he was seven. He looked at the picture they'd just hung that depicted soaring mountains and open skies. The vistas he'd only see from the ground now. "Yeah, I loved it." No one knew how much. No one knew what a hole it left in his life.

"It was lucky you weren't more injured."

"I thought so at the time." He took another sip of coffee. Time to get going before the entire scene became maudlin.

"What do you mean?"

Looking at her again, he shook his head. "Since I was a kid, I wanted to fly. I busted my ass to get the grades needed for the Academy. Studied like no one I knew to get in, to stay in. Flying was all I thought it would be and more. It wasn't just controlling the power of the plane, it was the feeling of unutterable freedom I felt, so far above the earth. Of feeling one with the thrust that kicked in and pushed the aircraft across the sky at incredible speeds. It was, I don't know, almost magical."

He closed his mouth. Hell, he sounded like some damned poet. She'd probably burst out laughing.

"And nothing else is magical?" she asked.

He shook his head even as the thought of Friday night rose. It had almost been magical with Caitlin. Was that why he wanted another time with her? To see if he could capture some kind of magic?

Slamming down the coffee cup, he rose. He'd never shared those thoughts with anyone else. He wasn't going to stay and be seduced into revealing other aspects of his life to some young innocent with wide blue eyes and soft sympathy. Time to head for home. A few insults with his brother, and life would regain its balance. Be back on track.

"Are you leaving?" Caitlin asked when he picked up his hat.

"Looks like it, unless this was enough getting-to-know-you time and you're inviting me to stay the night."

She shook her head.

"What are you doing here, Caitlin? Why Tumbleweed? Why Friday night?" he asked, turning the hat in his hands as he watched her.

"You had a dream and lived it for a while. You were lucky, Zach, no matter what you think now. You have those memories forever. No one can take them away. I have nothing. I was sick as a child. My parents are old, I was a late baby. They kept me from doing anything. Out of love, they said. Maybe, but if so, it was misguided. This is my one chance at freedom. I'm trying to find out who I am and where I fit into the greater scheme of things."

"And you came to Tumbleweed to do it? Seems to me there are other places closer to Maryland."

"Maybe, but I had an offer of a job and a friend—Joan."

"You've been here, what, a week now? Find your way yet?"

She shook her head. "But I'm trying. I'm exploring different things."

"Like Friday night." He'd just been part of an experiment?

Shrugging, she nodded. "I told you I didn't want a long-term relationship. You don't either. We hurt no one, right?"

He smiled sardonically. "That's debatable. Don't sell yourself so short, sweetheart. You deserve more than a one-night stand."

"Maybe. But it sure widened my horizons."

"Being *nice* and all."

She laughed softly. "Sorry if that rankles. I'll try for another word."

"I'd settle for another chance."

Catching her breath audibly she stared at him.

"If you ever see your way clear, you let me know." He placed his hat on his head, pulling the rim low.

"I will."

Time he got out of here. And in the future, he'd stay away from naive virgins!

"I'm becoming addicted to cowboys," Caitlin murmured Friday night when she pulled her car into the parking lot at the Oasis Bar. Twice last weekend and already back for another fix, hoping to find the delight in dancing and meeting new people she found on her first visit. Lindsay had insisted she join the group tonight. Joan had other plans, but didn't even try to warn Caitlin away. She'd just told her to have fun.

Tomorrow all the teachers were going to a neighboring town to watch the local high school football game. But tonight they were out to party.

For a sheltered woman from Maryland, the change seemed extraordinary. And one she could grow used to. But, learning from the first time, she brought her own car. No way was any cowboy going to take her home. She would manage by herself. She was smarter after last week in many ways. One-night stands left a person feeling discontented and unsatisfied…and yearning for something that was indescribable. She had tried it and not liked it as much as she'd thought. Next time, she would wait until there was some caring between her and her partner. If there even was a next time.

But she doubted anyone would be like Zach Haller. Brushing her fingertips across her lips, she could almost imagine she still felt his kiss from Wednesday. His pushing her toward a repeat of their time in bed gave her a shivering thrill. But he hadn't been serious, or he would have tried harder. Not that she'd have given in, but the thought tempted.

Caitlin did not expect to see Zach tonight. After last Saturday's fiasco, she doubted he would ever show his face in town again. They hadn't mentioned Margot when he'd helped her hang her pictures. What had the two of them resolved? Too bad he wouldn't be here tonight—no one danced like that cowboy.

Pushing into the bar, she hesitated a moment, looking for her new friends. Still feeling shy, she scanned the room. Spotting Lindsay, Caitlin raised her chin and headed for the table, plastering a wide smile on her face. The place was as crowded as last weekend and as smoky and as loud. Was it quiet during the week, or always popular?

Almost stumbling, Caitlin spotted Zach leaning against the bar, arrogantly surveying the room. He had a beer in one hand and was talking to the man next to him as his gaze roamed. Astonished that he'd have the nerve to show up tonight, she quickly looked away—almost as if she were ashamed to know him. Which wasn't true. She had loved last Friday night. She'd felt special and exciting in a way only a sexy man could make a woman feel.

Their time together Wednesday had given her a better understanding of him. He'd lost his dream, something he'd worked hard for over the years. No one seemed to see that or cut him any slack because of it. Was that one reason he was so wild? Looking for something to make up for the lost magic? Were the people in town so blind? Or used to seeing what they wanted, what they expected? To them, he was the rowdy cowboy who got into mischief as a kid.

But Wednesday had been a moment out of time, not the beginning of a long and fruitful relationship. She had to remember that and stop thinking about him!

Lindsay indicated a chair and smiled her greeting. "So how did your first week go? I know on Thursday morning you mentioned you were still in the honeymoon stage, but that ends fast with kids. Tired?"

Caitlin sat down and nodded. "But in a good way. I

probably won't stay late tonight, even though it's fun to be around adults for a change.'' She acknowledged the three other teachers at the table.

Their laughter was good-natured and knowing.

"The dancing will pep you right up.''

"Or wear me out.'' Caitlin glanced casually toward the bar again. Zach's back was half to her. She didn't think he'd seen her yet. Would he ask her to dance tonight? Or had she made her position clear on Wednesday? Why waste time on her when someone like Anita might be more accommodating?

"I'm a bit surprised to see Zach Haller here tonight,'' Caitlin murmured to Lindsay as the band began another song.

Lindsay looked at the pool tables. "Yeah, well nothing fazes him for long. I wonder what he and Margot decided. I can't believe the nerve of the man trying to deny what had to be obvious. Why would she lie?''

Caitlin followed Lindsay's gaze to the pool tables—and saw Zach. Startled, she swiveled around to stare at the man at the bar. Was she seeing double? Or was that his brother? Were they twins?

"I thought the man at the bar was Zach,'' she said, confused.

Lindsay shook her head. "No, that's Sam Haller, Zach's older brother. Two years older, I think. Not that he's any better than Zach. Wild boys, those Hallers.''

Wild and very much alike. Caitlin stared. If Zach had not slept with Margot, had it been his brother? Why would she lie and name Zach? And why had he said there was no one in town Margot could have confused him with? It didn't make sense. And Caitlin was a person who liked everything to fall in line.

The band played loudly. The sound of boots on the wooden floor almost drowned out the conversations behind him as Zach leaned over to make a shot. He'd come to town just to show he wasn't going to be intimidated by Margot's accusations. He was not the father, though now he had a good idea who was—Sam. He had been at the party that night, though he'd come late. Not that it mattered. Zach's hands were tied, unless he wished to damage his brother's chances at gaining joint custody of his son, Greg.

Angry as he'd been when he learned Sam had married Alissa, Zach would do nothing to harm the son they'd produced. Greg was a cute kid. Zach had seen him a couple of times from a distance. It was too soon after their betrayal to want to get to know his nephew. If things had been different, he and Alissa would have had a child by now, maybe more than one.

But it wasn't Greg's fault his parents were cheats and liars, and Zach wished the kid a better relationship with his father than he'd had.

Blowing the shot, he took the teasing from Freddie Lambert and stood back while Freddie took his turn. Idly glancing around, Zach spotted Caitlin Delany. Suddenly the commotion of the bar faded into the background. She sat surrounded by teachers at a table near the door. He smiled cynically. Maybe he would ask her to dance again. She'd been an armful last week. One he still hadn't forgotten. Not in dancing or in bed. Would she give in after another round of dances?

A movement at the bar caught his eye and he looked right into the smug gaze of his brother. Sam grinned, raised a long-neck bottle and then pushed away, heading for Caitlin's table. Zach watched impassively as Sam closed in on Caitlin. Unable to hear the exchange, Zach knew Sam was asking her to dance. He wanted to throw down the cue and storm across the room, cut out his brother and make sure Caitlin danced with him. Only him. Instead, he tightened his grip on the stick and turned back to the game.

He was the man who took nothing seriously. He lived

life for the moment, and to hell with the consequences. It didn't matter to him who Caitlin danced with.

He'd tried going nose to nose with his brother over a woman once before and lost. He wasn't going to do it again. No one was worth that. He'd play a little pool. Maybe Anita would come by tonight. They could dance a little and perhaps he'd take her home. Or not. The thought didn't appeal like it once had.

Freddie missed his shot, looking up quickly to see if Zach was watching.

"My turn," Zach said mildly. It wasn't worth getting bent out of shape about Freddie's cheating. Hell, he should be used to it by now. Cheating at pool was a small thing, not like cheating in relationships.

Despite his unwanted interest, he refused to look up to see his brother dancing with Caitlin. It was bad enough his imagination had her in another man's arms. He didn't need to see the reality.

Six

Despite her intentions of staying only for a short time, Caitlin found her energy level rose with each dance. She was having a great time. Feeling like the belle of the ball, she danced with almost every man who asked more than once with several. Refusing to acknowledge that she yearned for a dance with the man at the pool table, Caitlin threw herself into each tune. Her popularity stemmed from the novelty of being the new woman in town, she knew, but it didn't matter. She flirted, practicing with her eyes and slow smiles. She laughed at jokes and parried invitations to slip outside for a few minutes. A steady diet of this would not appeal, but for tonight she was having a grand time.

Except for the dance with Sam Haller. When he'd first approached, she expected him to be much like his younger brother. But he wasn't.

She expected a lighthearted, outrageous flirtation. But he came across as strongly macho, a bit chauvinistic and definitely on the prowl. And Sam didn't miss a beat in deni-grating his younger brother. His scathing comments during their dance made Caitlin want to slap his face and tell him to shut up.

Instead, she made sure she didn't dance with him again. And it wasn't for lack of interest on Sam's part. He asked her several times. The third time she refused, Caitlin im-mediately accepted another cowboy, hoping he would re-ceive the message. She didn't like the man.

And for once she ignored her mother's dictates to always be polite. She was striving to be her own woman, and that did not include spending time with someone she disliked.

Not sure why she felt such strong dislike, she tried to analyze it while she sat out a dance to rest her feet. When did boots get broken in? When did they become so com-fortable no one wanted to throw them out? Probably when they were falling apart, she thought, rotating her ankles, trying to ease the soreness.

Sam was dancing with Anita, making a show of fancy steps. Anita seemed just as content dancing with Zach's brother as she might have been dancing with Zach.

Caitlin let her gaze drift to the pool table. Twice she'd caught Zach's eye while she'd been dancing. Once he had drifted by, holding some woman in a tight embrace, but the look on his face hadn't been happy or teasing. Not like she remembered.

Taking a final sip of her warm cola, Caitlin tapped her fingers in time to the music.

"We're about ready to call it a night. How about you?" Lindsay leaned over so she could be heard over the noise level of the band.

Caitlin was not ready to leave. She'd been thinking about it all night and decided she would have a dance with Zach Haller before she went home.

"Just about. See you on Monday. I'm going to make a stop in the ladies' room right now."

She escaped into the rest room and splashed water on her heated face. She'd stall until her fellow teachers left. If Zach wasn't going to ask her for a dance, she'd ask him. His distance had her confused. Given half a nod on Wednesday, he'd have taken her straight to bed. At least that had been her assessment. Now she wasn't so sure. Maybe he didn't want anything more to do with her.

One night without strings, then move on.

That suited her, except she didn't want to move on just yet. Had last Friday been different because it was her first time? Or was there something special about Zach that kept her off balance? Time to find out.

She pushed open the door and glanced around the room. Lindsay and the others had gone. Quite a few of the crowd had left. The smoke still hung in the air, and she knew her clothes and hair would reek later. But she was still captivated with the discovery she wouldn't suffer an asthma attack.

Zach stood by one of the pool tables, watching another man line up a shot.

Feeling daring and worldly and unlike the shy girl from Annapolis, Caitlin headed directly for him.

"Care to dance, Cowboy?" she asked.

Zach turned slowly and looked at her, his expression guarded. For an instant his eyes flickered to where his brother stood. Then back to Caitlin.

"I'm in the middle of a game."

"I can wait," she said.

"Hell, ma'am, he can go dance. Forfeit the game, Zach-o. I'm going to beat the pants off you, anyway," the other cowboy bragged.

"In your dreams," Zach responded, his eyes never leaving Caitlin's.

She felt that curious sensation deep inside when he looked at her—warm and soft and hungry all at once. Glancing at the other player before she made a fool of herself by reaching out to touch the man in front of her, she smiled. "Zach's pretty good, I've seen him play."

"Yeah, I bet you have, darlin', and not pool."

"Shut your mouth, Freddie, or I'll shut it for you," Zach said calmly.

Freddie looked surprised. "Sure thing, Zach. No need to get riled."

"Play."

She should have been insulted, Caitlin told herself, but inside she was laughing. Carefree and wild, that was her new persona. And it must be working. Zach's partner thought he had something for her. Did everyone in the room? While she didn't want her reputation tarnished, she couldn't help feeling a bit proud if people thought she was up to Zach's speed. Joan had told Caitlin he was way out of her league.

"Dance?" Sam came up to Caitlin and put his arm across her shoulders.

"No, thanks." She ducked away. "I'm watching the game."

"Fast action, huh, Zach?"

"Butt out, Sam." Zach leaned over and slammed the ball into the pocket. He moved to the next one, ignoring his brother. Caitlin wished she could. The tension was almost palpable between the two of them.

"Heard Margot Simmons is after you," Sam drawled, leaning against the edge of the table, his eyes tracking his brother. "Watch yourself around this guy, Caitlin. He can be forgetful, sometimes. Right, Zach? Like you forgot something important one night? And then forgot to shoulder your responsibilities?"

Zach straightened and looked directly at Sam. "You have enough problems on your own plate, you don't need mine."

"Too right, I don't. Just warning the newcomer."

"I don't need any warning. I make my own decisions,"

Caitlin protested. She wished Margot had shown up tonight. Maybe with the two brothers side by side, she and everyone else would wonder if her allegations were accurate—especially when Zach continued to refute them.

Zach knocked the last two balls in and tossed the cue on the felt. "Game, set and match. Thanks, Freddie."

"Damn lucky, that's what. Rematch?"

"Not tonight. I have a dance to claim." He pushed by Sam and caught Caitlin around the waist, leading her to the dance floor. The space was no longer crowded.

"Next time you want to start a feud, take an ad out in the paper," he muttered as he pulled Caitlin into his arms.

"What are you talking about?" she asked, instinctively snuggling closer. It felt different from all her other dances. Right, in a way she couldn't explain. Raising her arms, she encircled his neck, feeling his taut body along the length of hers. Thinking at once how right they were for each other, how well they fit together. Unbidden, the memory of their lovemaking bloomed. They had fit perfectly in bed, as well.

Glancing around casually, Caitlin saw no one was paying them any attention, except for Sam. His smoldering gaze never left. She turned away. Feeling as daring as she had last week, she smiled brightly up to Zach. Her life had been full of firsts for weeks. And every success emboldened her to strive for more. Feeling intoxicated by her own self-confidence, she tossed her head.

"So, when are you inviting me to see your ranch?" she asked.

Zach shook his head. "Probably never."

"Thought you might teach me to ride."

He closed his eyes and leaned his forehead against hers, his hat sheltering them from the lights overhead. "You know, Caitlin, some people use that term to describe another kind of ride," he murmured pulling her even tighter until she could feel his desire.

Heat instantly engulfed her. Closing her own eyes, it was all Caitlin could do to ignore her embarrassment and continue dancing. She wanted to run for her car and escape. How childish. She had thought she was a woman of the world now, on her own and capable of dealing with things. Instead, his mocking comment had her flushing and wanting to hide.

Swallowing hard, she slowly shook her head until he opened his eyes.

"What?"

"I wanted to learn to ride a horse. I had asthma as a child and wasn't allowed around animals. But as a girl I longed to ride Black Beauty or the Black Stallion."

"No problems now?"

"None," she said firmly. "So how about teaching me that kind of riding?"

The song was drawing to an end.

"Come tomorrow, then, and we'll see what you can do."

"Can't. I'm going to the football game with a group of teachers from school. Can I come Sunday afternoon?"

He nodded.

"I'll bring a picnic. You can teach me to ride—a horse— and we can go for a picnic. I can't believe how warm it is here in January. There's snow in Annapolis."

"It's usually warm year-round here. But we can get Blue Northers which will freeze your b— Freeze you to death."

The band stopped and announced a break.

Slowly Zach released her. "Thanks for the dance, Caitlin. You know your way to the ranch?"

"I'll find it."

He touched the rim of his hat. "Be seeing you, then." Turning, Zach left the bar.

Startled at his abrupt departure, Caitlin glanced around. Sam still stared at her. He took a step closer, and she fled. She'd had enough for the night, and bed sounded good to her.

Hearing hurried steps in the parking lot, Zach turned around to see Caitlin crossing to her car. He frowned. Didn't she have any sense? What would everyone think if they saw her leave with him a second weekend in a row? Especially with Margot blasting his reputation to kingdom come?

"What are you doing?" he asked when she reached him.

"Going home."

"Couldn't you have waited another few minutes?" he asked with asperity.

"Why?" Her blue eyes were so innocent he wanted to shelter her from life's harsh lessons. But he couldn't. No one could keep everyone safe forever. Some people just found out the hard facts of life earlier than others. He hated for her to lose that innocence, though.

"Why? Now just what do you suppose those people inside are going to think when we leave together. For the second time?"

She glanced over her shoulder and frowned. "Why should they think anything?"

"Leaving with the town's bad boy? Lady, they're going to smear your name from one end to another."

"I doubt it. Anyway, what I do with my life is my own business. And we aren't leaving together. We just happen to be leaving at the same time."

"Details that can be overlooked for a juicy bit of gossip. Go back inside for a few minutes."

"I'm going home. I think you are a bit paranoid. No one cares what we do."

"There shows the ignorance of a city girl. Small towns thrive on gossip. Don't play with fire."

"Or what?" she asked sassily.

Zach's temper flared. He knew she was deliberately provoking him. But after the last week, his disposition wasn't exactly calm.

"Or you can get in over your head," he said taking her

shoulders and backing her gently against the side of his truck. Before she could say a word, he kissed her. Not a gentle kiss, but a full-blown passionate kiss that did nothing to assuage his anger, but built the level of desire higher than ever.

She was warm and sweet and he couldn't get enough of her. He held her head, tilting it slightly to better reach the dark moistness of her mouth. He rubbed the silky texture of her hair, reveling in the soft sensations. After one startled moment, she responded. Instead of scaring her off, he'd somehow changed tactics. He wanted her, wanted her like no one before. The thought scared him. Hell, he couldn't get involved again. He'd been burned once and refused to succumb to the allure a second time.

But passion was different. It only involved bodies, not souls. And he craved this sweet body in his arms like nothing he'd ever known.

When he felt her hands pulling him closer, he knew he was lost. No sense fighting it, not when she wanted him just as strongly.

"Not here," he said, pulling back to kiss her throat. She smelled so sweet, like roses. She tasted uniquely Caitlin. And he began to think he was growing addicted to her taste. "We can be at your place in—"

"No." She pushed him away, breathing hard.

Zach looked at her, anger threatening to take over. "What are you doing, playing some kind of game?"

"No game." Lightly she brushed her fingers over her lips, shook her head as she warily stepped to the left, distancing herself.

"No games. Just a refusal. You can't be mad at me one moment and then expect me to jump in bed with you the next."

"It's not as if it would be anything new," he drawled, attacking.

She lifted her chin and stared haughtily at him. "*Nice* as it was, I'm not sure I'm ready to repeat that event."

He fisted his hands. She'd deliberately taunted him with the word. She knew he hated it.

The door to the bar opened and the noise and light spilled out to the parking lot. Zach swung around. Two couples were leaving. Behind them Sam stepped out.

"Hell, that's all I need. Get home, Caitlin," he said without looking at her.

She reached out and touched his arm. "Zach?"

He spun around. "I made a pass, you rebuffed it. End of discussion." He reached around her and opened the door to the truck and climbed inside. A quick glance at her convinced him she might not think she was playing games, but the end result was the same. He wanted her and she'd said no. Again.

Dammit! He hit the wheel and started the engine. Roaring off into the night brought no relief. What a joke. The first time he'd been interested in someone in a long time, and the woman didn't reciprocate.

Caitlin rolled down the window and let the warm Texas sunshine bathe her arm. It was a beautiful day. The sky was clear and so deep a blue it almost hurt. It reminded her of the painting she'd recently bought. Smiling in quiet anticipation, she turned up the radio until the country song blared across the Texas landscape.

Beside her on the front seat was a basket packed with as many different items as she could cram into it. She wanted this picnic to be the best ever. It was her first with a man. She tried to remember when she'd been young. Had she ever gone on a picnic with her parents? Probably not. They would have feared a problem. It was easier to stay near the oxygen and hospital than take chances.

She'd changed all that. Wondering at the chance meeting with her former doctor, she gave thanks again that it had happened. If she'd never found out, would she have ended up living her life as a quiet rendition of her mother? Never venturing out, never trying new things? Growing old without ever having lived?

No chance of that now, she thought. Life had been full of changes. And the most amazing thing—every one had been for the good. So far. She knew she would make mistakes. But she would learn from them and not repeat the same one twice.

Yesterday had proved to be totally different from her years in high school. Most of the teachers who went to the game had taught the team members when they'd been smaller. In a few years maybe some of the little boys in her class would be on the football team, and she'd have a vested interest in the games.

But the excitement of the match, the yelling of the crowds and the welcome given by her fellow teachers had been heady. She'd screamed with them, groaned when one of the players missed a pass and eaten hot dogs and popcorn until she was stuffed.

Another first. How many more were there?

Smiling, she saw the drive leading to the Lazy H Ranch. Where did they get the name? She didn't picture Zach as lazy. Couldn't picture any rancher succeeding if they didn't give it their all. She'd have to ask.

Slowing when she reached Zach's house, she wondered if she should have called to let him know when to expect her. He probably hadn't stuck around the house waiting.

Climbing out of the car, she headed for the front door. Knocked. Turning to study the scenery while she waited, she heard nothing from inside. The rolling hills were green, from the recent rain, she supposed. Cattle grazed on the hills beyond the driveway. White faces, reddish-brown bodies. Not black Angus—the only breed she could name.

The minutes ticked by. It was quiet but for the soft soughing of the breeze and the occasional lowing in the distance of one of the steers. The day seemed even warmer than in town. Was it because of the open fields? Where was Zach?

She returned to her car and continued up the drive. He'd said he lived about a mile from the main operations of the ranch. She'd just find the barn and maybe he'd be there already saddling their horses. Giddy anticipation filled her, as it had all morning. From the expected riding lesson? Or from seeing Zach again?

Cresting a small hill, she saw the ranch buildings spread out before her. To the right stood a huge dark gray barn with an open loft door showing the stacked hay. The double doors at ground level were both open, revealing only darkness within. To the left was an old home, mellowed over the years, looking as if it had grown up from the land on which it sat. Two shade trees offered a bit of respite from the sun.

As she drove toward the barn, she looked for Zach.

Stopping beside Zach's truck, Caitlin turned off the engine. Horses dozed in the corral; a windmill turned slowly, pumping water into a trough. She heard the sound of voices inside the barn. Heading that way, Caitlin recognized Zach's. And heard another say, "Don't reckon we'll be able to finish that before Wednesday."

"I said I want it finished by Monday," Sam replied, his tone harsh.

Caitlin paused in the doorway to let her eyes adjust to the dim light. There were several men standing near the center, facing Sam. Zach leaned negligently against one of the stall doors, watching the proceedings with a bored air.

"Can't be done, boss."

"Don't tell me that. If it isn't I'll find some hands who can do the work!"

"Sam," Zach warned.

"Shut up. If I want anything from you, I'll ask."

"Or take," Zach murmured. "Give it a break, Sam. The

men said it can't be done before Wednesday. There's nothing saying Wednesday won't do.''

"I say Wednesday won't do, and I'm the head of this outfit. You keep out of this.''

"You may be the boss, but you don't own the entire shooting match. Cut them a little slack.'' Zach's voice had an edge.

Caitlin hesitated. She didn't know whether to barge in or sneak back to her car and wait until the meeting was over. So far no one had noticed her. Discretion being the better part of valor, she decided to leave just as Zach straightened and looked at the opening.

A smile slowly lit his face.

"Do what you want, Sam, you will anyway. But if you jeopardize the rest of the season by firing good men, don't complain to me.''

He started walking toward Caitlin.

"Don't worry about the ranch, Zach. It's mine and I'll run it fine. Wouldn't want you to have to work when there's a woman around to play with.''

The tightening of his jaw showed Caitlin Zach was not unaffected by his brother's insult, but he didn't acknowledge it in any other manner.

"Hello, Caitlin,'' Zach said, taking her arm and turning her away from the gathering behind him. He drew her to the corral and looked down at her.

"Ready for that riding lesson?'' he drawled.

"Horseback riding,'' she said, wondering if she'd ever hear the word again without remembering his insinuations.

"What else?''

She looked at the horses in the corral. They looked bigger up close than from the car. Suddenly long-ago dreams of a younger Caitlin rose. She would grab the mane and throw herself up on the horse before he began to gallop across the wide-open meadow. Bareback, she and her mount would race the wind.

The reality might not prove to match the dream. But she would learn to ride. And maybe one day, she'd race the wind.

"I've been looking forward to it," she said politely.

He laughed softly. "You're quite a contradiction," he said, thoughtfully studying her.

"Why?" She looked at him and her breath caught. His skin was tanned from long hours in the sun, the crinkles around his eyes lighter in color as if he squinted to see the far distance. He'd been a pilot, how did he resign himself to being earthbound?

Wanting some kind of contact, she reached out to touch him, felt the rock-hard muscles clench when her fingers skimmed his arm. "Why am I a contradiction?" she repeated.

"Because one minute you're coming on like you're experienced, and the next you look at me with innocence shining from your eyes. You're better at this game playing than most women."

"Fooled you, I'm not playing games. What you see is what you get."

"And will I get you again, Caitlin?" he asked, moving closer, crowding her. Not that she minded precisely. But it was the middle of the day, and any minute all those cowboys inside could come pouring out.

"Thought we were discussing my learning to ride a horse," she stalled.

"Answer my question," he challenged.

"Maybe some day. But I want to explore—"

"Other men?" his voice came harsh.

"No!" That she knew. For a while at least she wanted to adjust to being her own woman. And how could she tell this man that none of the other men she'd met in Tumbleweed had come close to getting her interested? Had he spoiled her for all other men? Or would the novelty wear off soon and free her for other experiences? For the moment she couldn't imagine making love with another man, but time would certainly change that. Wouldn't it?

"Zach, if you're going to push for that, I'll go back home."

He turned and climbed the fence, jumping down inside the corral. "Go to the gate and open it. I'll get the horses." Snatching a couple of ropes from the top rail, he walked over to one horse and looped the rope loosely around his neck. The horse began to follow Zach. Catching a second the same way, he was soon heading for the gate. Caitlin fumbled with the latch, then swung it open. As soon as the horses were through, she shut it, afraid one of the others would try to escape.

Zach made quick work saddling both horses, explaining to her each step of the way. He made no more personal remarks, scarcely looked at her. Of course he was working, but Caitlin wished he'd at least glance at her once in a while.

The men came out of the barn a few minutes later, grumbling. One threatened to quit. Zach noticed, but remained silent. He seemed to grow angry with the situation. Caitlin wondered why he didn't stand up to his brother if he really thought Sam was handling things wrong. Weren't they both owners of the ranch? Though from Sam's comment, she might be wrong. Maybe he owned it all and Zach only worked on it.

"Ready to go?" Zach asked, slapping the stirrup down after tightening the cinch.

"Just like that?" she asked, looking at how high the saddle seemed.

"We'll walk around for a while, when you're ready, we'll try a faster gait. But you aren't going to learn standing there."

"What about our picnic?"

"Going on a picnic, huh, Zach-o," Sam said, standing in the open door to the barn. "And with yet another pretty woman. How many does that make this week?'' He looked at Caitlin and smiled. ''You watch yourself with him, darlin'. You'd be safer with me.''

''I don't think so,'' she said under her breath.

''Get the food, I'll carry it with me,'' Zach said, ignoring his brother.

By the time Caitlin brought the basket from her car, two of the cowboys had saddled horses and ridden off, dust swirling in their tracks. Sam stepped closer. She handed the basket to Zach and waited while he tied it onto the side of his saddle. He would have to help her up, she'd never make it by herself.

''I'll take care of you, darlin','' Sam said, assessing the situation. His hands on her waist were hard as he lifted her. Acting instinctively, she swung one leg over and found herself astride the horse. Sam pushed one boot into the stirrup. Zach was on the other side and settled her other boot in the second stirrup.

''How does that feel?'' he asked, glaring at his brother over the back of the horse.

''Fine, how should it feel?''

''Like your feet are in snug, and there's no play,'' Sam said, running his hands down her calf. Then he pushed her knee gently toward the saddle. ''Grip with your thighs, darlin', and hold on tight.'' He looked up at her and winked. ''Like you'd hold on in the night.''

''Back off, Sam.''

''Not a chance, little brother.''

Zach handed Caitlin the reins and swung himself up on his horse. ''Let's go.'' Settling his hat again, he urged his horse to walk. Caitlin's turned to follow.

It happened so fast, Caitlin didn't have a chance to be afraid. One moment she was on the ground, the next being lifted to the saddle and in the next already walking away from the barn. It took only another few minutes for her to catch on to the horse's rhythm.

She was riding! They weren't racing the wind, but it was enough for a start.

"What was that about with Sam?" she asked when she caught up with Zach. Envious of the easy way he rode, she wondered if she could ever become so confident on the back of a horse.

Zach frowned at her. "He was staking a claim."

"What?"

"This time he was letting me know he planned to move in."

"Move in on what?"

"On you."

"I don't even like him."

"Watch yourself, he can be charming when he chooses."

"I doubt it."

"He's done it before," Zach said. "This time he's more blatant."

"Did what?"

"Moved in on someone I was interested in. Only last time he stole my fiancée from me."

Seven

"**I** don't know the full story—what happened?" Caitlin asked, trying to keep her horse even with Zach's. Holding on for dear life, she concentrated on Zach Haller in an attempt to forget how far she was from the ground. It was not her business, but he'd opened the door. Maybe he'd answer some of the questions that had plagued her ever since she'd heard about the scandal.

"It's ancient history now."

"Tell me." Slowly she began to relax, to move with the horse. If she didn't fall, riding might be the fun she'd imagined as a teenager.

He glanced at her, then shrugged. "Hell, I'm surprised everyone in town hasn't already told you all the sordid details. Alissa and I were childhood sweethearts. Dated all through high school. She agreed to wait while I was at the Academy. When I graduated, we became engaged. She seemed to change from that point on. Nothing would do but a big wedding, so I agreed to wait a few months. My first orders were for Germany, so I headed for Europe while she stayed here to plan our wedding.''

Caitlin remembered the plane crash, hadn't that occurred in Germany?

"And?'' she prompted when he fell silent.

"And Sam moved in while I was away. Got her pregnant. They were married a couple of months later. Have a little boy who's a bit more than three now.'' The clipped tone gave nothing away.

Stunned, Caitlin didn't know what to say. How could his brother have done such a thing? Or Alissa for that matter?

"Why?'' she asked.

"Why what?''

"Why would your brother have done such a thing? I always thought families were loyal, closed ranks against outsiders. I used to yearn for a brother or sister—someone to stand with me against the world.''

"Yeah, well maybe in Brady Bunch families that works, but it's not been my experience.''

"There had to be a reason.''

"If you want a reason, try sex. He couldn't stay away from her.''

"It takes two,'' she pointed out gently, still puzzling out the situation.

"That was the hell of it. I thought she loved me.'' He gave a harsh laugh. "Young, idealistic men probably fall for that line more than anyone.''

"But now you know better,'' she said. She'd never been in love, but she had a vivid imagination and could empathize with the shock and hurt he must have felt at the time. Still felt?

"Right. There is no such thing as love. Lust, sure. But I haven't seen much caring and love in the world. It's a myth, thought up by women who want to put a glossy shine on plain old lust.''

Caitlin was silent for a long moment. Was love an illusion? A myth? She'd read about it in novels, but never experienced it. "Maybe you're right. My parents professed to love me, yet kept me a virtual prisoner all my life. What kind of love is that?"

He looked at her. "Why did they do that?"

"I told you I had asthma as a child. Actually I was quite ill, forever in and out of hospitals. I'm also a change-of-life baby. I know my parents had given up on having children when I arrived."

"So they coddled their only offspring?"

"You could say that. Smothered, more like."

"Understandable. You were probably very precious to them. They wanted to protect you. I can relate to that."

"What?" She eyed him suspiciously. Was he mocking her?

"Never mind. So what changed?"

"I ran into my former pediatrician a month or so ago, and he asked how I was doing and wasn't I glad that I had finally outgrown the asthma. Further delving into the situation proved that he'd informed my folks of that when I was a young teenager. They had never fully believed him and kept me from all the normal activities that girls go through. No dating, no strenuous activities like sports, no exploring the mall on the weekends with friends—I might catch something, you know. I didn't even get to go to my prom."

"That explains the backlash."

"What backlash?"

"You're cutting loose and making up for lost time, right? I wondered why someone as innocent as you took me home the first night."

"So?"

"So nothing. But it explains the innocence in your eyes, which contradicts your behavior."

Caitlin flushed to the roots of her hair. She knew he meant her wanton behavior. She'd explained she hadn't done anything like that before. Did it make any difference? If she had it to do over, would she change that Friday night? She doubted it. Even thinking about it kicked her heart rate into overdrive, caused her skin to tingle all over—every inch he'd touched and kissed and caressed.

Zach was right, it had been more than nice.

"You doing okay?" His look was sharp.

"Yes." She tilted her head, hoping she gave nothing away. He'd probably forgotten all about it while she fantasized over it endlessly.

"We can try a lope. It's an easy gait, like sitting in a rocking chair."

"Fast?" Suddenly her confidence wavered.

"Not as fast as a gallop. If you get scared, just holler and we'll stop." Quickly explaining how to ride at the lope, Zach then kicked his horse lightly. Caitlin followed suit, momentarily stunned at the jerk when her horse took off after his. But he'd been right. Following all his instructions, she found she enjoyed the sensation. For a moment she felt as if she were flying! It was as magical as she'd always imagined.

Zach headed for a rocky escarpment in the distance. Because of the fast pace he set, talking was impossible. Had he done it deliberately, Caitlin wondered. Was he already regretting his exchange of confidences? It couldn't be easy for a man to admit his fiancée had deserted him for another—especially his own brother. Why, she wondered, had the woman waited until they'd been engaged? She'd had all the time he was at the Academy to form an attachment to Sam.

Would she meet the woman today when they returned to the ranch? How awkward must it be for Zach to live on the same place as the woman he'd once loved? No wonder he raised a little hell when he went to town.

And maybe her suspicions about Sam were wrong. He wouldn't have slept with Margot if he were married, would he? But that didn't make sense. Zach told her Sam was interested in her. Had he and Alissa separated?

Zach drew in beneath a huge cottonwood at the edge of a grove of trees that offered shade. Beyond them water glimmered.

"This is a beautiful spot," Caitlin said as she caught her breath. Slowly she slid off the horse, holding on to the saddle until her legs felt stronger. The pool of water measured a dozen yards across and seemed twice as long, totally surrounded by rocks. She couldn't see where the water came from. Was it a spring?

"Is it a natural pool?"

"Catches the rainwater. Gets real shallow in late summer from evaporation. But the water's warm. Because it's relatively shallow, it soaks up the sunshine. Even during the coldest days, it feels warm. We could go swimming if you like. It's deep enough for that at this time of year."

She smiled finding the thought tantalizing. "I didn't bring a suit."

"Neither did I. So?" His gaze challenged her. "Don't tell me—after your revelation about your parents, my guess is you've never gone skinny-dipping."

Shaking her head, Caitlin's gaze flew to his. Was he suggesting—?

Zach smiled and stepped closer. Brushing the hair back from her cheeks, he leaned closer, his eyes twinkling with amusement. "Be a new experience for you. We'll eat, rest up a bit and give the sun a chance to warm the water to the max, then go swimming. What do you say?"

Caitlin swallowed, mesmerized by his eyes, by the image that sprang up in her mind. The two of them, naked as the other night, frolicking in the warm water. Would they just swim, or would he kiss her, run his hands over her skin, draw her closer and—

Blinking, she tried to control her racing heart. Willed herself to begin to breathe again.

"I don't think so."

"Why not? Thought you were out to cut loose and try things denied to you as a child."

"Like going to the mall or dating," she said breathlessly.

"So call this a date." He leaned closer, his lips brushing against hers. "No entanglements." He kissed her again. "No commitments." He kissed her again, his tongue touching her lips briefly. "Just two people sharing a day." His mouth fastened on hers and demanded a response.

Caitlin felt as if she were a puppet on a string, that someone else directed her movements as she stepped closer and brought her arms around Zach's neck. She snuggled close, opening her mouth, making herself available for whatever he wanted.

Shivering at the sensations that danced along her nerve endings, she reveled in her own latent power, the power to lure this exciting cowboy. She boldly made forays into his mouth, learning him, trying to sort through the myriad of impressions that flooded through her. His taste was unique, the moistness sensuous and captivating. Her heart raced; her body, pressed so closely against his, grew warmer than the sun. Maybe she should consider swimming just to cool off. No matter how warm the water, her body heat had to be hotter!

When he ended the kiss, it was to trail light nibbles along her jaw, across her cheek, until he reached her ear. A soft nip on her lobe had her knees buckling. She tightened her hold around his neck, wondering how long before she melted into a puddle at his feet.

Daringly, she kissed his face and moved to copy his actions by taking his lobe between her teeth, biting gently. His groan startled her. And brought home instantly her effect on him. She wasn't in this alone. The heat in her body turned up another degree.

"I want you, Caitlin," his low voice penetrated the hazy delight that engulfed her.

She went still, pushed back a little so she could see him. His eyes met hers, his gaze intense. With each step toward claiming her own life, her desperate need to prove something to her parents began to fade. She saw things more clearly. She and Zach had shared an explosive night, but she knew something had been missing. Maybe another time together would show her the difference, but maybe it wouldn't. She liked being with Zach, could grow to like being with him—maybe too much, since he'd made it perfectly clear he wanted no entanglements, no strings.

"It was nice, Zach, but I don't think—"

"Dammit, *nice* is a hell of a word to use what we found that night." Anger flashed in his eyes.

"And you're doing your best to change that, I know. But I've decided I need more than just another time exploring things. Next time I want more."

"Like what?"

She'd never been held so close to any man except Zach. It felt odd to be having this discussion still pressed against the length of his hard body. But she didn't want to move, just wanted to clarify her thoughts. Her fingers rubbed against his hair as she tried to formulate the words. His hat shaded their faces, and she could see the desire in his gaze.

"I don't know. I was really caught up in the moment last Friday, almost intoxicated with the notion of freedom. And I was feeling a bit rebellious against my parents. But next time I want it to be for me—not because I'm thumbing my nose at anyone."

"You used me?"

She smiled and nodded. "Yes, I did. Are you upset? We said no strings. You're not trying to change that now, are you?"

His eyes darkened, but he didn't look away. "No strings doesn't mean we can't make love again."

"I agree."

"You do?"

"Yes, but when I'm ready. It takes two, remember?"

"Yeah, just like with Sam and Alissa." He released her and stepped away, looking across the range.

Caitlin didn't like the feeling of abandonment that filled her. She wished he'd held her a little longer. "Were you terribly hurt?" Dumb question. If he loved her, of course he'd have been hurt. She didn't know how to hold conversations with men.

"When?"

"When she told you, of course."

He continued looking into the distance across the Texas landscape. The wildness of the scene made Caitlin feel they were alone in the world. Just the two of them. A bit like Adam and Eve, she thought fancifully while she waited for his reply.

"Yeah, of course I was hurt," he said at last. "I'd loved her for years, I thought. I couldn't believe she and my brother—"

The tight clenching of his jaw showed Caitlin more than the words that he still felt that hurt. How awful that the two people he'd thought had loved him the most had betrayed him.

"But you don't love her anymore?" She wanted that clarified. Wondered if he still longed for the woman. Wondered why it mattered to her.

"No." His gaze dropped back to hers. "I got over her a long time ago. Long before their divorce. When she wanted to take up with me again, I refused."

"They're divorced?" That explained Sam's behavior.

"After a couple of years. I think Sam made a play for her just to out score me and got caught up in the whole thing. That's what really burned me at the time. He'd known her all her life and only made a play for her after we got engaged."

"Not very nice of your brother, but then I don't think he's so nice, anyway."

Zach shrugged and slowly turned toward Caitlin.

"Ready to eat?"

So the subject was closed, she thought. Just as well. She had no business prying into his private life. That led the way for him to expect her to share her thoughts, and she was too confused right now to want to even try.

"Sure."

He turned and began to unbuckle the picnic basket from his saddle. "I didn't bring you here to rehash old history."

"Why did you bring me here? To make love again?" she asked, watching his efficient movements with the buckles. His hands were large, broad and calloused. She remembered the feel of them on her skin. Shivering despite the warmth of the day, she knew she wanted to feel his hands on her again.

He grinned. "I wouldn't say no, darlin', if you give the word."

"Don't call me darling. It's meaningless unless there is some caring between the people. Besides, your brother calls me that. I don't like it."

"For a sheltered young woman, you certainly know your own mind."

"And don't mind speaking it. I figure the world won't end if I stand up for myself. After twenty-four years of living someone else's idea of my life, it's past time I took a stand, don't you think?"

"Don't judge your parents so harshly, Caitlin. I'm sure they wanted the best for you. When you were sick as a little girl, they probably panicked with the thought of losing you. In retrospect, they could have done things differently, but cut them some slack, don't cut yourself off from them."

"Why not? They smothered me! I couldn't do anything I wanted and it was all for nought! There's nothing wrong with me. I've been in that cowboy bar three times now. There is so much smoke it would choke a horse, but I didn't have a single problem."

"You know your parents love you. Maybe a bit too strongly, but you have to admit their intentions were probably good. Don't cut them out forever."

"Are you so close to your parents?" she asked, not liking the direction the conversation had taken. She wanted to distance herself from Maryland and all that her life had been until she'd come to Texas. Not be told to become a dutiful daughter.

"My parents are dead," he said flatly. Carrying the picnic basket closer to the water, he hunkered down. "This suit you?"

"I have a light blanket in the basket. I thought we could sit on that," she said kneeling beside him to raise the lid.

A few minutes later she took a bite of the roast beef sandwich she'd prepared hours earlier. Gazing around, she let the peacefulness of the setting slowly invade her senses. The shade protected them from the sun. The dappled sparkles in the water caught the sunlight and reflected it in a million directions. She wondered just how warm that water was.

Zach's comments about skinny-dipping echoed. Wishing she was as casual about these things as he appeared to be, she turned to him.

"When did your parents die? Do you miss them?"

"My mother died when I was little. I can hardly remember her. I don't miss my old man."

"You two weren't close, I take it."

"No."

The silence stretched out for several minutes. Zach ate, pulled one of the sodas from the basket and popped the top. Drinking, he set the can on a rocky spot and looked at her. Sighing, he spoke.

"My father was really proud of his ranch. He loved it more than anything. As I mentioned the other day, he didn't like the idea of me going into the Air Force. Did all he

could to block it, as a matter of fact. But I was determined
to be a pilot.''

"Wasn't he excited when you were accepted? So few
are.''

"No. Didn't come to the Academy once while I was
there.''

"Not even for graduation?''

"No.''

"Oh, Zach.'' Caitlin's parents had been so proud of her
accomplishments in school. Despite their concerns for her
health, they had proudly done all they could to make her
own graduation a huge celebration. All the relatives had
been invited, the few friends she had from high school. The
party had been subdued compared to the cowboy bar, but
it had been fun. Caitlin couldn't imagine her parents not
attending her graduation.

Suddenly she questioned her own behavior. Deep inside
she wondered if what she was doing was right. She knew
her parents loved her. Overprotective, sure, but beneath that
there was a strong core of love. Her graduation ceremony
and party were only one example of their love for her. And
they weren't young anymore. Hadn't been young when
she'd been born. What if something happened to them before she saw them again?

The thought disturbed her. Maybe she could call them.
Just to let them know she was doing all right. Just to hear
their voices.

"Did you make these brownies?'' Zach asked taking a
bite.

She nodded. "When did your father die?'' she asked.
She really wanted to know about Zach. He was a contradiction, and she tried to understand why.

"About four years ago.''

"Zach, everything happened four years ago,'' she said
slowly.

He looked up. "It was a hell of a year.''

"You said your plane crashed while you were in Germany, your fiancée married your brother while you were in Germany. And that was four years ago. Were you still in Germany when your father died?"

His expression changed. "No. I'd returned home by then." Bitterness laced his voice. "He got what he wanted, both sons working his ranch. But he never forgave one for trying to escape."

"What do you mean?"

Zach crumpled the empty soda can in his hand. Taking a deep breath, his tone neutral, he said, "He left controlling interest of the ranch to Sam."

"But Sam is the older brother, isn't he? Isn't that what people do, leave the older one the most? In the olden days, the oldest got everything."

"He could leave it however he wanted. And he did. I have forty percent. And a house." He tossed the can into the basket. "Don't know why I stay."

"It's your home," she said softly.

"No, it's a place to live," he corrected. "Finish up and we can walk around. If we climb the rocks, there's a great view of the valley. Later you can tell me if you want to swim or not."

He hadn't forgotten, but there was nothing beguiling in his tone. It was totally take-it-or-leave-it. Caitlin gazed at the water again. It looked inviting. And crystal clear. Could she contemplate such a thing? Skinny-dipping. Visions of Tom Sawyer frolicking in the Mississippi. Shyly eyeing Zach, she knew she could not. Not in broad daylight, and not with this sexy cowboy.

Or could she?

Zach leaned back on his elbow and watched Caitlin pack up the picnic basket. She was neat and meticulous. Probably got that from her older parents. He wondered if she missed them yet. With all the care they'd showered on her as a child and young adult, he bet they missed her like crazy. How long would she hold out? She was too kind-hearted to stay estranged forever.

"Ready," she said, standing and brushing off her jeans. She looked at the water again. Rising slowly, Zach wondered what she was thinking—considering swimming? He almost laughed. He had a way to get her to go along—just get her mad enough to kick over the traces. Would it work?

"Come on. The view is great from the top." He set off. This was one of his favorite spots on the ranch. Sam knew about it, but not that it was a favorite. If he knew that, Zach was sure he'd do something to spoil it. Drain the water maybe, or haul carcasses over. It was a secret he'd keep. Maybe he should warn Caitlin to refrain from mentioning to Sam.

The rocks were worn smooth from the wind and rain. Occasionally there was a loose one, but the climb was easy—even in boots. Before long they stood on the top. Spread out before them lay the valley, green from the winter rain. Cattle grazed in the distance. Cottonwoods dotted the landscape—signs of water in an otherwise arid land.

"Wow, this is great. I bet we can see a hundred miles!" Caitlin came to stand beside him. Close enough Zach could smell her. Her scent caused the normal reaction when he was around her. He wanted her.

If he didn't stop putting himself in these situations, he would go crazy. Granted their one night together had been wild and wonderful. But unless he wooed the lady to overcome her resistance, one night would be all he'd get.

Which should have suited him fine. It's what he'd settled for over the past four years. He refused to get tangled up emotionally with another woman. In fact he didn't want to get attached to anything. Made it easier to move on if the need arose.

"Is all this your ranch?" she asked.

"Straight ahead and to the right it is. That narrow rise

over there marks the boundary with neighbors. Our ranch lies more in that direction,'' he said, sweeping his hand to the right.

"It's so much land. My parents have a nice small lot. Our backyard was more like a garden. And Maryland has so many trees you really can't see any distance. This is fantastic." Happily gazing toward the far horizon, Caitlin fell silent.

Zach drew in another deep breath and held it. For a moment life was perfect. He was surveying the land that was his beside a woman who knew how to keep quiet and enjoy the view. The perfect ending to today would be the two of them together in his bed.

Caitlin looked around. "We could sit over there, couldn't we? And just soak this up?"

"Sure."

She settled on the rock and smiled. "I like this. Maybe I should rent some property from you and your brother and build a house right here."

"Long way from electricity and running water," Zach commented, leaning back against one elbow, his eyes on the horizon. "Do me a favor, Caitlin. Don't tell Sam where we came today."

She looked surprised. "Okay. Why not?"

"He doesn't need to know everything." He wasn't going to tell her the real reason, she'd think he was nuts. But he wanted this spot kept just like it was.

"There's a lot of animosity between you two, isn't there?" she asked.

"You could say that."

"I can understand why you feel that way. Why is he mad at you? I mean, he got the girl, he got the ranch. Seems like he had everything his own way, and you're the one that had the setbacks."

"Setbacks?" He almost smiled at her whitewashing over things. It illustrated her naiveté, her innocence. God, he wished he still had that idealistic outlook he'd had so many years ago.

"You know what I mean."

"Ask him."

"I don't expect we'll ever be close enough for me to do that," she murmured.

"He's interested in you, Caitlin."

She looked at Zach. "To get back at you, don't you think?"

"Why wouldn't he want you for himself? You're pretty, different from the women we grew up with."

She smiled and leaned closer. "Yes, but I make it a policy to see only one brother per family."

"Since when?" God, she was pretty. Her cheeks were pink from the sun, her eyes sparkling and clear. She smelled like flowers on a spring morning. His gut tightened, and it took all his willpower to resist reaching out and dragging her into his arms.

"Since today. So you tell me—why the animosity?"

Zach shrugged. "Don't know really. I think at one point he was jealous of the choices I made. He's always been on the ranch—didn't go to college. Maybe he wanted to and couldn't. Things weren't this bad before I applied to the Academy."

She pushed his hat off and ran her fingers through his hair. "It's awfully hot up here, isn't it? I can't believe how warm it is for the end of January. At home we'd have snow."

"Enjoy it while you can." Reaching out, he captured one hand and laced his fingers through hers. Her palm was soft and warm, her fingers long and slender. He liked the feel of her skin against his. Wanted to feel that skin all over, have her run her hands over his body. Catch the fire they'd built that Friday night and burn away the memories of the past four years.

She took a deep breath. "If you turned your back when I got into and out of the water, I could try swimming."

The shock slammed through him. Instantly visions of her gleaming body streaming with water rose to mock him. He'd fantasized about her since he'd made love to her. Wished he had done it beneath the sun to miss nothing. His fingers and mouth knew her, but his eyes had seen little in the darkness of her bedroom.

"Then let's go swimming. I promise I won't look while you get into the water." Maybe she didn't realize how crystal clear the water was. Before the day was over, Zach would seduce this woman or go crazy in the attempt.

"Can I trust you?" she asked suspiciously.

He tried to look as innocent as he could manage. "Of course, why not?"

"You have a certain reputation in town."

"You wound me."

"But I think it's an exaggeration."

"What?" That caught him off guard. He sat up, resting one arm on a bent knee. He'd worked hard to create that reputation. People didn't pity a devil-may-care, arrogant cowboy.

"I think you project that wild-cowboy image." She tilted her head and studied him gravely. "But I've not seen anything to support it. No one can give me specific instances of your rowdy behavior. Tell me if I'm wrong."

"You're wrong. Don't forget Margot."

"You didn't father her baby. What have you done that's so wild?"

"Hey, girl, just because you don't see everything, doesn't mean it doesn't happen. I like to party, get drunk, sleep around. Raise hell."

Caitlin frowned and spread her fingers in front of her. Touching one finger with the tip of her other index finger, she began. "One, I've never seen you drunk. The night we spent together you had one beer. Two, I've seen Anita, but where are the legions of women you are supposed to have seduced and left? Three, you admitted you had not slept with Margot. Even for the sake of a bad reputation, you won't take on that. Four—''

His hand covered hers, bending her fingers into a fist.

''Shut up.''

She looked at him, waiting.

''I just promised not to look if we go swimming, but I have every intention of seeing as much of you as I can.''

Her laugher was soft and rich. ''Wow, that's really dastardly. I might want to see as much of you as I can. There's just the two of us here, and I didn't get to see as much as I wanted that night. You're my first, why wouldn't I be curious? But if you ever tell a soul, I'll deny it!''

He tapped her chin, not trusting himself to touch her more than that. His inclination was to pull her beneath him and kiss her until they both forgot their names. He'd even slipped a condom into his jeans that morning—just in case.

''I can't believe our upstanding schoolteacher would resort to lying.''

''Only if pushed. Let's go swimming.''

''Need a lesson on that?'' he asked as he rose and pulled her to her feet.

''I can swim. Learned at the Red Cross. As a lifesaving skill. My parents thought that was important—in case I was ever in a boat and it sank.''

''Do a lot of boating?'' he asked as they started down the rocky slope. His body ached to touch hers, his attention divided between the meaningless conversation and the image he could almost touch of them in the pool. Together. Naked.

''Nope,'' she said as they carefully made their way back down the rocks. ''Never even been in a boat. But my parents wanted me to be prepared.''

''So they prepared you for all eventualities.''

She stopped and shook her head, her gaze finding his. ''They did not prepare me for you!''

Eight

Zach went to check the horses. In the distance a trail of dust hung in the air. He waited for a moment, but didn't spot anything threatening. Making sure the horses had plenty of shade, he turned back and headed for the pool.

For a moment anticipation built. Urgency pressed against him. He wanted to be with her, see her bright blue eyes light up with amusement, hear her laughter. Learn more about her, who she was becoming.

He stopped suddenly, aware of danger. She was just a woman from town. He couldn't let her become important to him.

But it was hard to convince himself when he saw Caitlin beside the pool. She'd taken off her boots and was unbuttoning her shirt. For a moment he wanted to rail against fate. He'd been close once before, thought he had the world by the tail, but it had all ended. And he didn't trust any longer.

But this was no strings and no commitment. She was

exploring all the facets of becoming a woman, and who was he to deny her?

Caitlin heard his step on the rock and slowly turned, her fingers fumbling with the last button. She had hoped he'd take longer, give her the time and space she needed. Blood rushed through her veins, pounding in her ears. Excitement curled deep inside as she watched him walk closer. His eyes were shaded beneath the brim of his hat, but she didn't need to see them to know he was devouring her. She could feel it as if he touched every inch of her.

Her shirt was open, but not parted. Drawing in a deep breath, she could feel a hint of breeze cool the heated skin beneath her lacy camisole. Mesmerized by the man as he came closer and closer, she couldn't move, only concentrate on the fire that he'd begun and which now threatened to blaze out of control. She needed the water in the pool to quench the flame.

He stopped inches from her, tilting his head so his hat shaded her, as well. Trembling in trepidation and anticipation, Caitlin hoped he couldn't see how hard it was for her to be bold and brazen, when nothing in her life had prepared her for these overwhelming sensations. She took a breath and his scent filled her body. Licking suddenly dry lips, she gazed into his eyes.

Slowly Zach raised his hands and cradled her head, tilting her face up to his, as his mouth pressed against her lips. Warm and firm, his lips moved against hers, opening slightly as if to taste her. His tongue brushed against her lips, wetting them, teasing them. When she parted to respond, he continued to nibble. She wanted more. Clasping his wrists with her hands, she moved closer. He didn't react as she wished, but continued the soft kisses, sweet kisses, until she felt the world tilt and wondered if her knees would hold her.

Trailing his hands down her neck, she felt his hard calluses against the softness of her own skin. His touch electrified. He traced the column of her neck slowly, as if savoring every inch. She felt his fingers slide beneath the edge of her shirt, skimming over her shoulders, brushing back and forth as if he was fascinated by the texture of her skin. When the shirt slid off onto her arms, Caitlin lowered them to let the shirt fall to the rocky ground.

Glorious, she thought, reaching up to encircle his neck, her hands knocking off his hat. For a second the sudden sunlight almost blinded her, but she kept her eyes tightly closed. She wanted nothing to interfere with the melody playing in her body. Nothing to interrupt, to shorten the sensuous pleasures.

"You are so soft," Zach whispered as he kissed her neck, pausing on the pulse point at the base of her throat. The dampness on his lips transferred to her throat and the soft breeze cooled what he inflamed. "You'll like swimming nude. The water will feel like silk, just like you do. Moving against your skin as you swim, caressing every inch of you."

His husky tone intoxicated. She could have listened to his honeyed words forever.

When he slipped the satin strap down from the camisole she wore, Caitlin opened her eyes. His were closed, his lashes dark against his cheeks. Learning her by touch alone, he continued slowly moving his hands over her. The pebbles beneath her feet shifted as she tried to keep her balance. The world was spinning away, and she was flying. It was better than riding the horse, better even than that first night at her house.

"Touch me," he said, finding that delectable spot behind her ear that sent shivers down her spine.

Her hands moved to his broad shoulders, kneading the muscles softly, feeling his latent strength. Slipping one hand down his chest, she found the snaps of his Western shirt. The popping sound startled her, and she opened her eyes in surprise. If she weren't burning up with desire, she would have found it funny. But the impatience that grew had no time to be amused. She wanted to feel his skin, discover if he was as hot as she felt. Learn his body with her hands as he did hers.

How could she have forgotten? Sensory overload was the only explanation. That first time together had melted her brain circuits, and being awash in pleasure had not left room for conscious thoughts and memories. His chest was hard, muscular and dusted with a light covering of dark hair. Bringing her other hand down, Caitlin allowed herself the pleasure of running her fingertips over every inch. When she brushed one nipple, Zach groaned and caught her hand, pressing it tightly against his chest.

"I like that," he said, not releasing her fingers.

"I could do it again," she offered, intrigued by his reaction. Was it identical to what she felt when he thumbed her nipple? Dare she ask him?

"Not if you want to go swimming."

"Swimming?" Is that what she wanted? Or more, much more than that with Zach?

Holding her hand, his free hand cupped one breast, raising it beneath the camisole. He bent his head and opened his mouth over the tip, wetting the material, and sending shock waves coursing through Caitlin.

She sighed a moan of sheer pleasure. If she was about to burn up with his touch, she'd better get into the water soon. She needed it to cool her skin, bring her back to some semblance of sanity.

Zach raised his head, tilting it as he listened.

"Damn." He spun around and walked away, peering beyond the trees.

"What is it?"

"I think someone's coming."

"Oh, no!" Caitlin reached down to snatch her shirt. The sleeves were turned inside out. Struggling, she turned her back to the direction Zach stared. Why wouldn't the darn thing cooperate? She could hear the sound of horses now. Finally. Thrusting her arms into the shirt, she hurriedly buttoned it up to the neck. Reaching for her boots, she stomped into one and then the other. With a regretful glance at the pool, she ran her fingers through her hair, hoping it didn't look as messed up as it felt. Running her tongue over her lips, she tasted Zach and could feel her swollen lips.

"Who is it?"

He turned and looked at her, his shirt refastened. "I don't know yet. But they'll be here in a minute," he said, leaning over to pick up his hat. He slapped it against his thigh a couple of times and set it on his head, pulled down low. "So much for our swim."

Caitlin nodded, regret warring with embarrassment. It had to be some of the men who worked on the ranch. Well, what couldn't be changed had to be endured. Raising her head, she walked toward him. "Should we pack up?"

"Might as well." He walked to the picnic basket and was still folding the blanket when two riders came around the trees and stopped.

One Caitlin didn't know, but she recognized Zach's brother instantly. Caitlin wondered if Zach felt as disappointed as she. Their afternoon was over, one way or the other.

Sam reined in and leaned on the saddle horn, surveying his brother and Caitlin. No sense being angry at him, she thought, he didn't know what he was interrupting.

"Saw your tracks," he said, looking over at the pool. "Forgot this was here."

"Sorry we already ate, there's nothing left," Caitlin said when Zach remained silent. "We were just getting ready to leave."

"Tired of this guy's company already?"

She shook her head.

"What do you want, Sam? This is a private party," Zach said.

"Pedro and I were riding fence. Told you I wanted that patch near the McCullough's spread fixed before the end of the week."

"McCullough's spread is nowhere near here."

"So? It's open range, after all, Zach."

"And very nice, too. Zach showed me from the top of the rocks. You have a huge place," Caitlin said politely, trying to defuse the tension.

"Maybe Sam can show you the rest of the ranch," Zach said avoiding her eyes.

Caitlin turned, unable to believe he'd said that. Was he trying to foist her off on his brother? After the scathing things he'd said earlier?

"What's wrong with you showing me around?" she asked, standing up for herself. She'd had a lifetime of people telling her what to do.

"I have things to do back at the house," Zach said carelessly, striding to his horse.

Puzzled, Caitlin followed, watching as he untied his mount. She copied him and stood near the saddle, as if trying to figure out how to mount. Zach dropped his reins and closed the distance between them. Before Caitlin could protest, he picked her up and tossed her into the saddle. "Have fun with Sam," he said.

"Zach!"

Ignoring her, he swung onto his horse and kicked it savagely. Furious, he headed away from the escarpment.

Caitlin almost followed, but she knew she couldn't stay on a horse going that fast. Swinging her gaze around, she looked at Sam and Pedro. "Was that your intent? Drive him away and ruin my afternoon?" she asked calmly. She would not give away her feelings before this Haller any more than she did before Zach. Anger burned deep. Both at Zach and at his brother. She should have stayed home.

Sam smiled and motioned to Pedro. "Now, darlin', I don't believe your afternoon is ruined. I can show you around just as easily as Zach. Makes more sense—the ranch is mine.''

"I'll take off, boss, and finish the fence line," Pedro said, looking at Caitlin and touching the brim of his hat.

"Just check things out today, Pedro. I'll send a crew tomorrow to repair any breaks."

Caitlin tugged experimentally on the reins, gratified to have the horse respond as she wanted. She could walk back, but she wasn't sure she was up to anything faster. Annoyed with both Sam and Zach, the sooner she left for home, the better!

"You don't have to be in such a hurry to leave, Caitlin. Come on, I'll show you some other areas that are as pretty as this one."

"No, thank you."

She was not going to argue with the man. She didn't even want to be with him. Damn Zach, anyway, for leaving her. The move caught her by surprise. "I have to get back," she said, heading in the same direction Zach had. She could see the dust trail in the air left by his horse. Would it be enough to guide her back to the ranch house? Or would it begin to settle long before she could see the barn?

"Stick with me, darlin', and I'll show you a better time than Zach. He's too wild for you," Sam said.

"How so?" Maybe she could get Sam to give her some examples. So far nothing she'd heard supported Zach's wild reputation. After the lies her parents had told she was wary of trusting anything she couldn't see with her own eyes.

"What?"

"How is he too wild for me? Give me an example or two," she said waspishly. She was so tired of people telling her things for her own good. She would decide for herself. And maybe stray from the straight and narrow if that was her choice.

With a regretful glance back at the pool, she sighed. Her first skinny-dip would have to wait.

"I didn't come out here to talk about Zach."

"Then why did you come?"

"To check on the fencing."

"Don't let me keep you. I'm sure I can find my way back."

He reached out and grabbed the reins, drawing her horse to a halt. "Not so fast. You can't be in a hurry, you'd planned to spend the day with my brother. He left, what's stopping you from spending the rest of the afternoon with me? I'll show you around, and then we could get dinner in town later. I'll make sure you get home before bedtime."

The thundering of a hard-ridden horse came to her ears. Caitlin turned away from Sam, a smile breaking out on her face. Zach had almost reached them. He'd returned. She was conscious of the rising excitement that gripped her. He sat on the horse as if he were part of him. She couldn't see his features beneath the hat, but her heart kicked into high gear. If she was so adamant about no strings, why did she react to this one man unlike any other?

"Didn't expect you back, Zach," Sam drawled when his brother joined them.

"Figured as much." He turned to Caitlin. "Sometimes my temper gets the better of me. But I've never walked out on a date before and I see no reason to start today."

"No problem, bro. I can take care of Caitlin," Sam taunted.

Caitlin looked at first one brother then the other. "We're going about this all wrong," she said. "Sam is the one who should be leaving. We had plans, if I recall."

Zach nodded then looked at Sam. "Move on."

"Hey, bro, this is my ranch. I have every right to be wherever I want on the place."

"You're intruding. Take a hike, *bro*."

"Now just what would those plans be? You don't want to get involved with Zach, Caitlin. Look at Margot."

Caitlin couldn't believe Sam had insinuated what he had.

Tilting her chin, she glared at him. "I think I should ask Margot," she said, sitting tall in the saddle. "I should ask her exactly what she remembers about that night and about the man who slept with her. To see if she can truly say it was Zach."

"One example of his wild ways," Sam added, glancing at his brother.

"Only I never slept with her," Zach replied evenly.

For a moment Sam held perfectly still. Then he eased back in his saddle and pulled his hat lower on his face. "Watch yourself, Caitlin," he growled. Kicking his mount, he took off. Dust rose in his wake, but he never looked back.

Zach watched until Sam was out of sight. Caitlin sighed softly and urged her horse toward the house.

"Where are you going?" Zach asked, coming alongside.

"Home. I think I've had enough."

He kept pace. "Thought we were going swimming."

"I'm not sure I could have done that, as enticing as it sounded," she said, careful to avoid looking at the man lest all her good intentions fled. She might not have gone swimming, but what else would she have been doing if Sam and Pedro hadn't arrived?

"Another time?" he said several minutes later.

"Maybe. I think I should get home. I have lesson plans to review before tomorrow."

They rode back to the barn in total silence. Caitlin refused to let her disappointment take control. She enjoyed the earlier part of the day, and it was enough. Nothing was perfect. Now she needed some time for herself. The roiling emotions that threatened to overwhelm her centered on Zach Haller. Being with him short-circuited her brain, and she needed to clear her head.

He was unlike anyone she'd ever known, and she still wasn't sure if that was good or bad. She wanted more when they were together, wanted to know more about him, about how he felt with the bad breaks he'd taken. Wanted to know his plans for the future. Wanted to see if her plans and his—

She slammed away from that thought. Infatuation, that's all, with the first sexy man to pay her any serious attention. It didn't mean she was falling for him. She had too many things she wanted to accomplish before tying herself down.

When they reached the barn, Zach called to one of the cowboys loafing in the shade and handed him the reins. "Take care of the horses, will you?" he asked.

He walked with her to her car. "Give me a lift home?"

"If you want. How did you get here?"

He opened the door for her and waited until he joined her in the car before replying. "I drove my truck. I'll walk back later and get it."

His place was less than a mile from the barn, only minutes away.

"Want to come in?" he asked when they reached his house.

She hesitated, knowing she should chalk up the entire day to a lost cause and head for home. She could review the lessons for the week, try to remember each of the children in her class, do her laundry.

"Yes, I'd like to come inside." Seeing Zach's house was much more interesting than dealing with lesson plans. And she couldn't deny the anticipation that danced along her veins. Maybe swimming was delayed, but they'd be private in his place, and he might kiss her again.

Feeling bold, brazen, barely able to contain herself, Caitlin entered the house of the wild and wicked cowboy. And stopped in surprise. He had more books in his living room than she'd ever owned.

"Good grief, it looks like a library!" she exclaimed.

"I like to read," he said, almost defensively.

"Me, too, but I get most of my books from the library."

"They don't carry all of these. Want something to drink?"

"Iced tea if you have it or a soda."

When Zach left, she crossed to the long bookcase beneath the window and read the titles of the books. Most dealt with cattle, breeding, ranching and agriculture. At the end of the top row were a handful of novels, mostly action adventure.

Studying the room while she waited, she couldn't believe he'd lived here for four years. It was as impersonal as a motel room. More so, maybe. There were no paintings on the walls, no photographs anywhere. Just sturdy furniture, a couple of tables, a small television and rows and rows of books.

Zach returned carrying a glass of soda in one hand and a long-neck beer in the other. He handed her the soda. "No tea."

"This is fine." Taking a sip, she looked back at the books. "Your reading material isn't very varied."

He shrugged and tossed his hat on one of the tables, running his fingers through his hair. "Thought I'd read up on ranching. I didn't study it in college, so I needed to catch up."

Sympathy flooded her. He'd never thought he'd end up a rancher. He'd planned to be a pilot, to spend his life flying in the stratosphere. But when that ended, he'd applied himself to learning about what he would be doing.

"You are a fraud," she stated, swinging around to face him. "I bet no one in town knows how hard you apply yourself. There's talk all over about your rowdy ways, but nothing concrete. The only thing people can say is how you soaped the windows of a bunch of cars when you were a teenager, and something about red food dye in some fountain. Teenage pranks, if you ask me. Yet you do nothing to dispel this reputation of yours. If anything, you encourage it. Why?"

"Pop psychology now?"

"I took some courses at the university. So, what's the real story here, cowboy?"

"Nothing. What you see is what you get."

"I don't think so." Caitlin finished her soda and handed him the glass. "I'm going home. Thank you for showing me the pool. I still want to go swimming sometime."

He put down the drinks and walked with her to the door. "Stay," he said.

She shook her head. "Too dangerous."

Slowly he smiled. "Sounds promising."

She laughed and reached out to touch him, dropping her hand before making contact. "It would be nice, wouldn't it?"

"Damn, not nice. Anything but that!"

She laughed again. "I think that's all you want, a chance to get me to change my description."

"What I want is another chance to get you," he stated clearly, his eyes gazing directly into hers.

Swallowing, Caitlin nodded. "Forewarned is forearmed. Goodbye." She left quickly, before she could change her mind. He didn't make it easy, nor did her own clamoring instincts.

He walked out with her and watched as she got into her car.

"There's an open house at the school on Wednesday, want to come?" she called.

"Not my thing. I don't have any kids," Zach replied.

"It's open to the town. After all, your taxes help support the school." She waved and drove off, her senses spinning. A truly liberated woman would have followed up on his invitation and stayed the rest of the afternoon. And maybe the night.

So much for having emancipated herself. She still had a long way to go. But each event moved her away from the sheltered life her parents had pressed on her. At the thought nostalgia threatened her. Zach was right, they had loved her, but they'd gone overboard. She missed them.

Zach watched the car drive away and turned back to the house. He'd walk up later and get his truck, but there was no rush—it wasn't going anywhere. He closed the door and headed for the bottle of beer. Caitlin's scent still lingered in the air—flowery, like roses. What would it be like to come home every day and see her? Share dinner together, talk about what they'd done during the day? What would it be like to know she cared about him like he was beginning to care about her?

Sex. That was all. He didn't trust women. Especially innocent ones who were just spreading their wings. She'd flirt for a while, then move on to the next man. She had been clear about not wanting any commitments, nor strings. At least she was honest in that regard.

And if he were as honest, he'd admit she was starting to matter—more than he wanted. The solution was to stay away from her. She'd find another sucker soon and that would be the end of it. Heading for the kitchen, he pitched the empty bottle into the trash and pulled another from the refrigerator. Time he got back to shoring up his reputation.

Caitlin called Joan when she reached home.

"I'm surprised to hear from you," Joan said. "Thought you might have plans for the weekend. Did you enjoy the game last night?"

"I sure did. I never went to football games when I was in high school. I, um, need some help."

"You've got it. I called your mother the other day and told her you were fine and that I would not be used to spy on you."

"Thanks, Joan. I appreciate that." Joan had been one of her few friends at college—content to meet for lunch and coffee and not questioning why she couldn't do more. "I want to stay friends. Your friendship has always meant a lot to me."

"Me, too. What help do you need?"

Caitlin took a deep breath. "I want to know everything you know about Zach Haller."

"What?"

"Everything, names, dates, all the terrible things he's done. But start from the time he got out of the Air Force. I don't care about teenage pranks. I want to know what he does now that is so awful."

"Caitlin, you're not still seeing him? God, he eats people like you for breakfast. Don't let his attention turn your head. As I told you, he's the love 'em and leave 'em type."

"Specifics, please." She would not admit even to herself that she felt anything for the man beyond a crush, a brief infatuation that would burn itself out quickly if she was lucky. And if she knew the real man, it would help.

It didn't help. The specifics were nonexistent. Unable to come up with a single incident, except for Margot's accusation, Joan sounded puzzled.

"I don't get it," she said some time later. "I know he's wild as a mustang, but I can't think of anything else."

Caitlin nodded. Just as she'd suspected. What was Zach's game? Why foster such a reputation when there was nothing to back it up? What purpose did it serve? She didn't know, but she meant to find out.

"I'm not quitting until I find out," Caitlin said.

"You might try Melissa, she's friends with Ted Burrows who was a good friend of Zach's when they were in high school. Ted works in Austin now, but he might know something and have told Melissa."

"Or there's nothing there but smoke," Caitlin said slowly.

Nine

Zach stopped the engine and sat staring at the schoolhouse. He'd spent twelve years in the Tumbleweed school system, the first six in this building. He wondered if Mrs. Savalac still taught fifth grade. He'd heard Mrs. Crosby had retired, and Miss Evans had long ago moved away and gotten married.

Hell, what was he doing here? Cars and trucks continued to turn into the parking lot. It would be full soon. He was just taking up space. Leaning back, he watched as parents hurried from their vehicles, heading for the doors that stood wide, light spilling out over the walkway.

Catching a glimpse of a couple he knew, he tilted his hat lower, obscuring his face. Marc and Cissy had two school-aged girls. He'd gone to school with Marc. It was hard to believe his children were already in school. If he and Alissa had married, any children they might have had would still be too young to attend elementary school. In a couple more years would they have been part of the parental gang wandering around the school?

He reached for the key. He could be far away in seconds. No one would ever know he'd come.

Instead, he withdrew the key and slid from the truck. He'd worn his new jeans, the shirt he'd picked up in San Angelo a few weeks ago and a bolo tie. He didn't know how dressy this event was supposed to be, but a man couldn't go wrong with what he wore tonight.

Feeling like a bull in a china shop, Zach walked up the path.

"Zach?"

He stopped, turned—and almost groaned when he saw Pete and Sally Hawkins.

"It is you! What are you doing here?" Sally said, hurrying to catch up with him.

"Thought I'd check the place out. My taxes help pay for the school, you know," he said, cringing. He knew the excuse sounded as lame to them as it did to him.

Sally giggled. "I guess they do. Somehow I never thought I'd see you checking out how your tax dollars were spent."

He shrugged. Sally had giggled through high school, still did, it seemed. He wondered how Pete stood it.

"Come to the first grade, our Susan has artwork displayed," Sally said.

"I might do that." Especially since Caitlin taught the only first-grade class—and she was the sole reason he was here.

Following the Hawkins, Zach tried to pretend he belonged, that he didn't feel like the world's biggest idiot. Just because Caitlin had invited him was no reason for him to show up. Since Sunday, he'd wondered what her classroom looked like, what she looked like when she stood in the front instructing children. He would have loved having a teacher like her, he bet. And it wasn't only curiosity about her classroom. He was fast becoming fascinated by every facet of the woman. What a contradiction. Shy and innocent in one breath, then bold and sexy. No telling what she'd be up to next, but he wanted to be there to find out.

Entering the classroom, he didn't immediately see her. The disappointment was sharp. Then he spotted her in the midst of several couples, probably answering questions about their kids. He glanced around. The chairs were tiny, the tables would hit his knees. Even the bulletin boards and blackboard were hung low. Perfect for little kids, but he felt like Gulliver.

"Here's Susan's painting. We'll have to hang this one, honey," Sally said, pointing out a multicolor blob.

Zach nodded and looked at Pete, a question in his eyes. Did Pete have a clue what the poster-paint-covered sheet was supposed to be?

Pete shook his head, then smiled at his wife. "We sure will, honey." Winking at Zach, he moved with Sally when she went to speak to Caitlin.

Zach hung back, leaned against the wall, crossing his arms and watching the woman he'd driven into town on a Wednesday night to see. The skirt that skimmed her hips looked soft and feminine as it swayed when she moved. The lacy top she wore emphasized the delicate swell of her breasts and set off her faint tan. Her blond hair had been brushed until it glowed like moonbeams. Suddenly Zach longed to feel it again, to run his fingers through its softness and let the silky strands tangle against his skin.

Feeling the familiar tug of attraction that was becoming expected whenever he came near Caitlin, he shifted his position and studied the room. Looking back when he felt Caitlin's gaze, he noted her surprise, then the warmth in her eyes when she smiled brightly.

Excusing herself from the small group of parents, she crossed the room quickly.

"Hi," she said. "I'm so glad you came. Want a grand tour?"

"Don't you have to answer to parents first?" He was conscious of the speculative looks they were receiving. If she weren't careful, gossips would have a field day with her reputation.

She glanced around. "I've spoken to everyone here. Latecomers can look me up if they wish." When she faced him again, her smile had not dimmed. "I see you're admiring our artwork." Gesturing to the paintings he leaned against, she shyly met his eyes. "What do you think?"

"Susan Hawkins did that one," he pointed. "I'm still trying to figure out what it is."

"It really doesn't matter, what's important is that they have fun and develop some sense of color and composition."

"She got the color part right," he said eyeing the bright yellow and red that splashed across the paper.

"Come on, I'll show you around."

Though the room was small, it took them a long time to make the circuit. Caitlin proudly displayed the reading area with the books her children could look at during quiet time. She explained how she taught the beginning readers and how she made sure all the children got a good basic grounding in the alphabet and phonics.

"Zach? What are you doing here?" A tall cowboy, dressed as if he'd just come from the range stopped him. "Evening, Miss Delany. I'm Tom March, Danny's dad."

"Hello, Mr. March. So glad you could come. Have you seen Danny's painting?"

"Uh, no. I saw Zach and couldn't believe he was here. Must be for your nephew, huh? I heard Sam's trying to get custody. Didn't think he was school-age, though."

Caitlin looked at Zach with some curiosity, then smiled warmly at Tom March. "Actually, I think Zach's here at my invitation. I wanted him to see where I work."

"Oh?" The cowboy looked from one to the other, speculation rising. "I see."

"Nothing to see," Zach growled. "Check out the paintings. I think I saw a horse done by Danny. At least it looked sort of like a horse."

When Tom ambled across the classroom, Zach turned his back on the room, glaring at Caitlin. "That was dumb."

"What was?"

"Saying I came to see where you worked. Don't you have a clue yet about the gossip around town? The last thing you want is to be linked with me."

"Why is that? What I do on my off time is my business."

"I don't think the good parents of Tumbleweed would relish knowing their kids were being taught by some notorious woman."

She smiled. "That being me?" she asked, her eyes brimming with fun.

"If you hang out with me, that'll be you."

"I hardly think your visiting the classroom on open house night constitutes hanging out with you."

"It will if you tell all-and-sundry you invited me. Tom's got the right idea, I could say I'm here for my nephew."

"Is Sam really seeking custody?"

"Yes. He wants it full-time, but I'm sure Alissa won't give that. But if he could get half a year or something, I think he'd be satisfied. He loves his kid, whatever else his faults."

"Miss Delany?"

Caitlin smiled at another set of parents. "I'll be right there." Turning to Zach, she made a face. "Duty calls. Will you stay until the end? We could go for coffee or dessert or something."

He hesitated a long moment. The temptation was strong. The only dessert he'd want would be her. And he could imagine her face if he told her that. Still, he could spend a few hours with Caitlin before heading to the ranch. And how much trouble could they get into at a coffee shop?

"What time does this shindig end?"

"Should be over at eight thirty. I really have to mingle. So I'll see you afterward? You might want to look at the other rooms."

"I'll wait in the truck," he replied. He'd seen enough of the school. And the odd feelings that welled up confused him. Would he ever want a family enough, trust someone enough, to risk marriage? He watched Caitlin as she greeted late-arriving parents and proudly showed off her classroom. He'd stay just a bit longer to watch her. No need to rush to the truck—there was nothing there he wanted.

Caitlin surreptitiously checked the large clock over the blackboard. Only fifteen minutes to go. Her cheeks ached from smiling. Nodding as she listened to Mrs. Parker go on and on about how brilliant little Nikki was, she tried to concentrate. But her attention was constantly diverted by Zach's presence. He hadn't left for his truck, but positioned himself against the wall near the cubbyholes and tracked her every move. She felt as if she were going crazy. It was as if she could feel his eyes on her, feel the magical attraction that shimmered between them. Which made it difficult to concentrate on her students' parents!

This was her first open house as a teacher. She liked her young students and was proud of their accomplishments. By the end of the year, she knew she would have made a difference in twenty-five lives. She should take every opportunity to get to know the parents, to explain her methods and her goals for the children in her class. But her body sang and her attention wavered more than once as she let her glance drift to Zach and then away.

He smiled and winked once, flustering her to no end. That melting sensation deep inside almost made her close her door early and hurry him away from the school.

Twelve minutes now. Smiling, she tried to catch the thread of the conversation. For a man who said he didn't want their names linked, he made sure there could be no other topic of conversation. She felt a tingling awareness that she wouldn't mind being linked with him in any number of ways—including a very intimate one.

God, now she was fantasizing images while she was supposed to be acting as a teacher!

"I'll certainly keep that in mind, Mrs. Parker," she said, when the woman wound down. Satisfied, the mother nodded, looking slyly at Zach. "What's Zach Haller doing here? I noticed him when I first came in. He doesn't have any kids—none born yet. Wonder what he's planning to do about Margot Simmons. Ought to marry her, I say. Terrible scandal for Tumbleweed, don't you think?"

A curious sensation feeling oddly like despair gripped Caitlin. Zach married to Margot? She wanted to shout a denial. Prudently she kept her head. "It was good to discuss Nikki with you, Mrs. Parker. Thanks for coming tonight." Nodding in farewell, Caitlin turned and looked at the clock. Thankfully only seven minutes remained until she could usher the parents from the room and close her door. According to Joan, the principal would announce the end of the evening on the PA system. Caitlin could hardly wait. With another quick scan of the classroom, she knew she'd spoken with everyone present.

It was enough.

She crossed to Zach. "Almost over. Once the announcement comes, I can close up."

"If you handle the kids like you handled the parents, you must be a hell of a good teacher," he said.

Flushing with pleasure, she beamed at him. "What a nice thing to say! I do my best. I love teaching. Though, if you had asked me before Thanksgiving, I would have given odds I'd never make it."

"You call your parents since you've been here?" he asked.

"No." She turned slightly so she could keep an eye on the room. It was easier than meeting his gaze.

"Don't leave it too late, Caitlin."

"Don't be telling me what to do," she flared up. Was it that he was right that made her so angry? Was it guilt? Or were her emotions just on edge because of Zach, because she was building dreams over the coffee they'd soon share? Could she entice him for more? Dare she even think thoughts like that? Was she ready for more? Ready to—

His finger tapped her chin, and she glared at him.

"Mighty prickly. Just an observation."

"So maybe I can observe, too. Stop acting like a rowdy cowboy and people would take you seriously."

"I'm doing just fine."

"Right. Which is why half the people here tonight warned me against you."

"Damn, I shouldn't have come." He glared at the few remaining parents.

"I think—"

The announcement on the PA system interrupted. The principal thanked the parents for attending the open house and urged them all to join the PTA if they had not already done so. The few remaining couples began drifting from the classroom.

"It's over. Thank you for coming," Caitlin said as she moved to the door.

Zach stayed where he was until the last mother left. "Ready for that coffee?" he asked, pushing away from the wall and walking toward Caitlin.

He reminded her of a predator and she was lunch, she thought whimsically. "In just a minute," she said, feeling the anticipation grow.

It was ten minutes by the time Caitlin had straightened the room and was ready to leave. The parking lot remained full; groups of parents stood talking and laughing. The open house was a good way to see friends and neighbors, Caitlin realized. She hadn't expected the crowd to still be here. Throwing caution to the wind, she linked her arm with Zach's. She had no reason to be ashamed of being seen with Zach Haller. And it was time everyone knew it.

"Playing with fire, little teacher," he murmured.

"I'm on my own time now," she replied, waving at Joan. Her friend looked at them and slowly shook her head. Caitlin just grinned. She knew Joan disapproved, but after their talk last weekend, Joan also wondered about the truth. As had Melissa after talking with Caitlin.

"Solly's is a quiet place," Zach said as they reached the edge of the parking lot. "Do you know where that is?"

"No."

"You can follow me, then."

"I didn't drive," she said.

"How did you expect to get home?"

"I thought you might take me."

"Pretty sure of yourself, weren't you?" There was an edge to his voice. But Caitlin refused to become intimidated.

"Just hopeful. If you hadn't come, I would have asked Joan for a lift."

Zach pulled his hat lower and headed for the truck, ignoring the clusters of parents.

Caitlin had to walk swiftly to keep up with him. She hoped she didn't have to break into a jog—how undignified for a schoolteacher. Then she smiled to herself. She had allied herself with the town's notorious bachelor, and she was worried about her dignity in jogging across the parking lot?

He opened the passenger-side door and waited until she was settled before shutting it. When he got in behind the wheel, Caitlin continued.

"Because, you see, I figured if you came tonight that would show me you were interested in me."

"Interested? Babe, we've slept together. What more do you need, to show I'm interested?"

"In me, not just my body. I don't think that first time should count. I was trying to prove something and you just picked up the new kid on the block. Though it was nice." She added the last just to tease him. Ever since Sunday, she'd been dreaming about this man. Fantasizing about ways to meet him, spend time with him. And more than one night she'd awakened after an especially erotic dream about Zach.

"My being here tonight probably ruined your reputation." Zach started the engine, revved it once, then took off.

"I doubt it. I think people were interested in your being here tonight, but as Mr. March said, they probably all thought you were there for your nephew. Do you see him often?"

"Tom?"

"No, your nephew."

Zach's hands gripped the wheel tighter. Caitlin found his actions curious.

"No."

"Why not?"

"Figure it out yourself. He should have been my son."

"But you're still not hung up on Alissa?"

For a long moment Caitlin thought he wouldn't answer. Although he'd already told her he'd gotten over Alissa a long time ago, Caitlin wanted to be sure. It was one thing to become interested in a man who was fancy-free—something entirely different if he was still in love with another woman.

"No, I'm not still hung up on Alissa," he said at last, an odd note in his voice. Had he just realized that?

"Then why haven't you got a girl? Unless you count Anita?"

"I don't need a girl. I do just fine by myself."

"Everyone needs someone," she said reasonably. "I yearned for a boyfriend when I was a teenager. Even in college. I dated a few times, but because I thought I was sick, I didn't let anything develop into a strong relationship. I thought it unfair to the guy."

"It's safer to go alone."

The revelation of his words stunned her. For a moment she couldn't figure out what he meant, then realized, though he denied any lasting trauma from his fiancée's betrayal, he must have been hurt beyond belief—especially when his brother also betrayed him. No wonder he wanted to remain a loner. He was correct—it was safer to be alone. He might not have the fun of companionship, but there was no danger of betrayal.

Caitlin recognized the café when Zach pulled into the parking lot. "I've eaten here before," she said. "When I first came to town. Their apple pie is yummy."

They found a booth to the side. The restaurant was not crowded, a few scattered couples, one table of six. Once they gave their order, Caitlin looked expectantly at Zach.

"Know what I think?" she asked.

He looked back, shaking his head slowly. "I haven't a clue."

She raised her fingers to tick off her points. "First, you aren't who you try to convince everyone you are. Second, it's time you got on with your life. You had a hard knock or two, but you're young, healthy and smart. Three,—"

"Third," he interrupted.

"Huh?"

"If you are going to say first and second, third is next. Otherwise you need to say one, two and three."

"Are you trying to change the subject," she inquired politely.

He nodded. "I don't need your pop psychology."

She frowned. "You said you wanted me."

"No secret."

Caitlin looked at him for a long moment. Then bravely said, "What if I want you, too?"

His gaze narrowed as he studied her. "Then I'd say let's blow this place and head for yours."

She rubbed the edge of the table, her gaze on her fingers. "You know, Zach, my folks have been married for forty-two years, eighteen before I came. One thing I've always found so wonderful about them is the love the two of them share. My dad still looks at my mom like she hung the sun. And she gazes at him sometimes as if he could walk on water."

Zach leaned back. "If you are looking for happy-ever-after, you came to the wrong man. I told you before, babe, it's no strings only. I'm not—"

"Chicken," she said brazenly, raising her eyes to gaze directly into his.

"What?"

Color stained her cheeks, but she didn't waver. "I said you're chicken. Once Burned Twice Shy, I can understand. But you flat out refuse to even give someone a chance. Not that it has to be me. Maybe Margot or Anita or any one of the other women in town. But you're shortchanging yourself by not allowing past hurts to fade and finding someone you could love and build a life with."

"I didn't bring you here for a lecture, Caitlin," he said tightly.

"Why did you bring me here?"

He leaned forward, reaching across the table to take her hand and hold it. "I came to soften you up so you'd invite me back to your place tonight. I want you. I thought once would be enough, but it wasn't."

"You just want to change 'nice,'" she said, breathlessly. His touch short-circuited every function—breathing, thinking, circulation. Another night with Zach? What could it hurt? She knew him better, liked what she knew, wanted him with a fever that amazed her. They were two single adults. Another night together would mean—

Would mean that she'd have another chance at that wondrous experience he'd shown her a few weeks ago. And a chance to make inroads into his own heart?

"What I want is to touch you all over that silky body of yours. To run my hands over your breasts and your stomach and your thighs. To taste your sweet mouth again, to plunge into your warmth and forget who I am and what I'm doing with my life. I want to smell that fragrant perfume you wear and have it rub off on me so I can still smell it in the morning. I want your body to hum for mine, to reach that plateau we found last time, maybe go higher. Thinking about you at night is about to drive me crazy. It's time we fish or cut bait."

"If I say no, you'll never ask again?" Thrilled at the words, amazed at the roiling sensations that crashed through her body, she could scarcely sit still, much less think coherently. It sounded as if he wanted her almost as much as she yearned for him.

"I won't be able to, I'll be stark raving insane!"

Slowly Caitlin smiled, hoping it looked sexy, hoping it was driving Zach as crazy as he said. Never in a million years had she expected to have such an effect on a man. Especially someone like Zach.

"Well, cowboy, if you want to try your luck again—"

"Two apple pies and coffee." The waitress placed the plates before them and then slapped down the mugs. Coffee spilled from Zach's. "I'll leave the check, pay as you go out."

Caitlin looked at her, knowing the moment had been shattered. Pulling her hand free in embarrassment, she picked up her fork and cut a small bite of pie.

"She says that every time, about pay as you leave. Think

she'd know anyone who has eaten here more than once would remember,'' Caitlin murmured.

''What's it to be, Caitlin?''

''Well, that's romantic,'' she said, toying with the piece of apple pie. Finally she took a bite. Cinnamon, apple and sugar burst on her tongue—and tasted like dust. She pushed the plate away. Unable to concentrate on anything but Zach, she knew the pie was a lost cause.

''So where do we go from there?''

''From where?''

''If you come back to my place tonight and stay, where do we go from there? You've said no strings so many times, I'm wondering if that's your middle name. Maybe I want some strings. Maybe I want all the things I didn't get to have as a teen, like dating and hanging out with a guy, and kisses and holding hands at the movies. The whole nine yards. What if I want more than you do, Zach?''

''Not my style, babe. You know my terms, take 'em or leave 'em.''

Caitlin nodded, her smile feeling wobbly on her face. ''I guess I'll have to leave them, then. And it's a shame, because I really am crazy about you, cowboy.''

She sipped her coffee and blinked her eyes. She would not cry! For heaven's sake, she was a grown woman. Not everything could always go her way. She'd probably fall in love a dozen times before finding the man she wanted to share her life with.

Fall in love? Where had that come from? She didn't love Zach Haller. She didn't!

Ten

Zach frowned as he slowed to turn onto the street that led to Caitlin's house. Staying had been a mistake. He should have left immediately after he'd seen her classroom. Hell, he should never have come into town tonight to begin with. But he could rectify that. They'd be at her place in just a few minutes, and he could explain it had been a mistake. Then leave.

But for a moment the words she'd said at the coffee shop echoed. And he wished for a second that he could give her what she wanted. Could offer dates to the movies, take her dancing on Friday and Saturday nights, kiss and cuddle and make love until this burning need for the woman finally eased.

Instead, once he dropped her tonight, he would stop seeing her. Not strictly true. He'd probably run into her around town in the months and years to come. If she stayed.

And he'd have to see her with some other man. He tightened his grip on the wheel. He'd been through that once.

He'd had to live with knowing Alissa and Sam had become a couple. He'd had to learn to unlove the woman he'd loved for years. It would be easier with Caitlin. He didn't love her. He'd only met her a few weeks ago.

On the other hand, maybe she had a point. Was he going to continue to deny himself companionship and sex because of Alissa and Sam? He could have an affair with Caitlin. It didn't mean forever. And he wouldn't get tangled up with emotions. Keep his heart safe for the time they split.

He pulled the truck to the curb in front of her house and stopped.

"I can manage from here, you don't need to get out," she said, already opening the door.

He caught her arm. "I'll walk you upstairs."

"No, thanks."

Fumbling with the key using his left hand, he shut off the engine, his right hand firmly wrapped around her arm. "I insist."

For a moment her eyes met his, then she looked away. "My mother would be so proud of your manners," she said scathingly.

"I don't care about your mother or my manners. I just care about you!"

She looked at him in surprise. "You do?"

Slowly Zach slid his hand down her arm until he caught her hand. Lacing his fingers through hers, he tightened his grip. He didn't know what the future held, but for this moment in time he wasn't willing to gamble it didn't hold Caitlin. And if he let her go tonight, that would end any chance he had for her.

He knew better than to expect happy-ever-after. That was fairy-tale material. But he could offer to stick around for a little while. Give her what she missed growing up. It wouldn't take long, he knew, for her to grow disillusioned and look for someone else. But for the weeks it did take, he could enjoy spending time with her. Take all the kisses he could store up, and be ready when she found someone else.

"No strings, but we could have an affair. I'd be faithful for as long as it lasted, if you'd grant me the same favor."

"An affair?" Her eyes shone in the streetlight.

He almost groaned at the excitement that danced in her eyes. "Most people would be insulted, or want more," he said in exasperation.

"Why? I've never embarked on an affair before. It sounds exciting. You really want to do that? With me?"

"Yes, I really want that." It was true. Why hadn't he thought of it before? They'd both know the terms going in, so no hurt feelings when it ended.

He felt a clutch of trepidation. *He didn't want it to end.* Time enough later to deal with that.

"So is that a yes?" he asked, trying to figure out what he'd do if she said no.

"Yes, thank you, I'm happy to accept. And I promise to be faithful," she said solemnly. Then she yanked his arm. "Are you nuts? Why would I want anyone else when I can have you?"

The jolt of pleasure surprised him. "I'll come up, then."

"And stay the night?" The breathlessness in her voice hit him hard. She wasn't afraid, was she? She couldn't be. They'd already done this once. This time it would better. Or at least he sure hoped it would be, though it was hard to imagine. The last time had been magical. Thinking about it made him want her so badly he was about to explode.

"I'll stay awhile, anyway." He wouldn't stay the night. But he'd tell her that later, when it was time to leave.

Her hand gripped his tightly. "I'm a bit nervous," she confessed, looking out of the windshield.

"I thought you liked it."

"I did. But I'm such a novice. And last time I was in a temper, rebelling against my parents and Joan's spying. I'm not sure I'll be very good at this."

He released her hand and got out of the truck and went to her door. "Come on, babe, I'll take care of everything."

Caitlin slid from the truck, surprised to find her knees worked. She felt soft and fragile, excited and scared all at the same time. Bravely walking toward the house, she hoped she did everything right. She didn't want Zach to decide after tonight that maybe she wasn't worth all the effort.

"Hey, not so fast." He caught up with her and threw his arm around her shoulders. "You look as if you are marching to a battle."

"No, just upstairs." Great, Caitlin thought, she should be looking soft and seductive. Instead, Zach thought she looked like a soldier. Taking a deep breath, she considered maybe she wasn't ready to embark on an affair. Maybe she needed a little more experience.

That was dumb. Not one of the men she'd met since arriving in Tumbleweed had appealed to her. None except Zach. And she already had some experience with him. For a second his kisses by the pool flooded her memory. What was she worried about? She loved being with him, liked what he did to her with his mouth, his hands. She couldn't wait.

But Zach had other ideas. Once inside her apartment, she turned, expecting him to sweep her into his arms and carry her to the bedroom. Instead, he tossed his hat onto a table and walked toward the kitchen. "Got something to drink? We didn't finish the coffee. Visiting an open house makes me thirsty."

"I don't have anything but soda," she said slowly, puzzled. Was she missing something? Hadn't he come up to go to bed?

"I was thinking more like coffee."

"Oh."

He looked at her. "Something wrong?"

Caitlin shook her head. "I'm surprised. I thought

we'd—'' Now she felt like an idiot. Maybe she did need more practice before this. A few nights with a man she didn't care about and maybe she'd get the basics down so she'd come across as polished, sure of herself. But since no one else appealed to her, she'd blown any chance of getting more experience before agreeing to Zach's proposal.

Zach closed the cupboard door and crossed the kitchen to her. ''Caitlin, give me a little credit. I thought I'd try to show some finesse, rather than tear off your clothes and carry you instantly to bed. If we are going to have an affair, we don't have to treat this as a one-night stand. We have lots of time.''

''I just thought that you wanted to and was surprised when you asked for coffee.'' She felt like a total fool. Turning, she tried to gain a bit of control over her emotions. Zach was right, they didn't have to do everything in the next five minutes. An affair implied a long-term relationship.

He tilted up her chin. ''I do want to. We can skip coffee if you like.'' His voice was low and sexy, his eyes gazed into hers and for a moment Caitlin forgot the topic of discussion. She loved it when he looked at her like that. Actually she loved it however he looked at her.

She nodded, boldly stepping into his arms. Offering her mouth, she closed her eyes when his head began to descend. The press of his lips on hers was as familiar as her face in the mirror. Sighing softly, Caitlin gave herself up to the magic of his kiss.

His scent filled her. His touch sent shivers down her back. His strong body seemed to wrap her up in both safety and razor-edged excitement. How that could be she couldn't fathom. Maybe when she could again think.

But right now all she wanted to do was feel. Feel the warmth of his lips, the moist roughness of his tongue as he explored her mouth, danced with her own tongue, beguiled her into his mouth where the explorations were all new. She felt alive as never before. The cascading sensations that built hotter with each passing moment stunned her. She'd thought she would remember, but it all seemed new and fresh.

"The thing about an affair," he said against her mouth, as his hands pulled her lacy blouse from her skirt and slipped beneath it to touch her bare skin, "is that we can make love wherever we want." His kiss about stole her breath. "In the kitchen, in the living room." Slowly he began to back them up until she felt the carpet beneath her feet. "Or in the bedroom." Her head spinning, she could scarcely understand what he was saying.

"Are we going to try them all?" she asked, her own hands fervently seeking the taut, hot skin beneath his shirt. She fumbled at the buttons. Why couldn't he have worn the shirt with snaps?

"Count on it. But tonight..." He kissed her jaw, found the pulse point at the base of her throat and kissed it. "Tonight, let's try the bed again. At least the first time."

Her knees wouldn't work. Her voice wouldn't work. She just hoped her heart could stand the pounding and not give out in the middle of the most exciting night of her life!

Trying again, she managed to whisper, "The first time?"

"I have a half dozen condoms in my pocket," he murmured, his hands now tangled in her hair, tilting her face back so he could kiss beneath her jaw, trailing kisses to that sensitive spot by her ear, tugging gently with his teeth on her earlobe. And every moment he massaged her scalp, ran his fingers through her hair as if fascinated by the silky texture of the strands.

"Oh!" *Six times?* Could she live through something like that? If not, what a way to die!

"You walk too slowly." Zach dropped his hands and scooped her up, holding her against his chest.

The room spun around, and Caitlin grabbed hold of his neck for balance. "I'm too heavy."

"Naw, you don't weigh any more than a bale of hay."

She laughed and groaned and leaned her forehead against his jaw. "Be still my heart. Your romantic words will turn my head."

"No romantic words, just the truth," he said as he carried her into her bedroom.

Slowly he lowered her legs until she stood. Linking his hands behind her back, he brought her snug against his body. The sensations were intoxicating. Caitlin kept her arms looped around his neck, pressing up against him in the remembered moves from their first time together.

"I like this," she said softly, kissing his chin, his jaw. Letting her tongue taste his slightly salty skin, she boldly mimicked his kisses.

Zach groaned softly and tightened his hold. Caitlin felt a thrill at the thought she could bring him the same pleasure he brought her.

"This is the part where you tear my clothes off," she said, her hands impatient.

"Who's running this seduction, you or me?" Zach murmured, opening his mouth over her skin.

"Both, maybe?"

He slowly filled his hands with her hair, rubbing the silky tresses between his fingers and looking at her in the scant light coming in from the living room. "I want to take this real slow, don't you?"

"I don't know. I'm about to melt into a puddle right now," she said, already feeling cooler without his eager mouth on hers.

Zach smiled and brought one hand between them to slowly unbutton her lacy blouse. His roughened skin caught against the lace, snagged and pulled, but he didn't stop. One button released and Caitlin stepped back an inch to allow his hand room to keep moving. She brought her own around and began to unfasten his buttons, matching him one for one, brushing her fingers against the warmth of his chest.

He released another, brushing his knuckles against her breast as he slid his hand inside her blouse while he worked the button through the hole.

She looked up. Was he teasing? Boldly following his lead, she again grazed her fingertips against the warm skin of his chest. Then she forgot the game. She wanted to explore those muscles again, feel the crinkling hair against her palm, against her breasts.

"Hurry," she whispered, unfastening the buttons as fast as she could manage.

In only seconds both were bare to the waist and Zach bent to kiss her throat, moving his open mouth across her skin, dampening it, chilling it, inflaming her. Kissing the tops of her breasts, he moved down slowly, tasting every inch as he moved closer and closer to a thrusting peak that ached for his touch. Licking her nipple, blowing on it, teasing was more than Caitlin could stand. She rubbed against him, pulled him closer, silently urging him for more.

When his lips closed over the rosy tip, she sighed and closed her eyes to fully enjoy the exquisite excitement that was only a foretaste of what was to come.

It was the same, yet different from before. She knew Zach better, liked what she knew about him, loved what he did with her. Did he feel this way with everyone, or was this as special for him as for her?

He tugged on the zipper of her skirt and Caitlin was distracted. Quickly releasing the fastening, she wiggled her hips until the soft material slid to the floor. His belt was impossible to unfasten, and she finally stepped back in frustration.

"Next time come in Velcro fasteners, it'll be easier," she muttered, trying to see what she was doing in the dark. "This is where my inexperience shows," she grumbled.

Zach laughed and took both her hands in one of his and held them while he quickly undid the belt and his jeans. In seconds they pooled at his feet. Struggling with his boots he grew impatient to get to bed.

Clothes shed, he scooped her up and laid her on the silky coverlet.

He handed her a warm foil-wrapped packet. "Are you ready or shall we continue this a while longer," he asked, his hands everywhere. Caitlin was almost frantic with need and desire and didn't want to wait another minute.

"Can you do it?" Zach asked, his mouth leaving soft nibbles on her belly, moving up to kiss the underside of one breast, then across to the other.

"You know better than anyone that I've never done this before." Caitlin squirmed to the side and sat up. She opened the packet and looked at him. Before she even thought, she launched herself at him and met him breast to chest. "I can't learn to do that now. I want you. You're driving me up the wall!"

Zach quickly donned the condom and turned her on her back. His kisses became deeper as his hand moved to the apex of her thighs. The gentle caresses only built the need. Caitlin wanted him now. She tried to communicate that fact through her own gestures as she attempted to pull him on top of her. Glad how smart cowboys were, she sighed in temporary relief when he spread her legs and entered slowly. But the relief was short-lived as the craving exploded. They'd done this before, and there was more. Savoring every moment, she moved with him, touched him and kissed him until the final moment. Almost consumed by the spiraling sensations, she hugged him tightly and held on for the rest of the ride.

This was Zach, her Zach. The stubborn, contradictory, wounded-in-heart cowboy that she loved.

Gradually the world untilted. Caitlin opened her eyes and looked up into his dear face. Smiling dreamily, she traced

the muscles of his back with her fingertips. He rested on
his elbows, keeping most of his weight from her. She
wanted to snuggle closer to keep the heat between them,
but she was already beginning to grow cool.

Zach kissed her gently. Moving to the side, he clasped
her and rolled them until he was on his back. Their legs
tangled for a minute, then she stretched out on top of him.

"Mmm, nice."

He groaned.

"Well it was. Very nice. Spectacular, even."

"Spectacular, I like."

"Mmm." Resting her cheek against his, she closed her
eyes. It was different when she cared for the person. And
right now she was afraid she was letting herself care too
much. How long did affairs last? He'd said nothing about
the future, committed to nothing really beyond tonight.
Surely he meant to stick around a little longer.

Her heart began to beat in fear, not excitement.

"Sleepy?" his voice asked as his hand swept over her
bottom, up her side, back down and then up her back.
Slowly, smoothly, rhythmically, he caressed her. She felt
like a cat and wished she could purr.

"A little, aren't you?"

"Yes."

"Are you staying the night?"

"No, I'll go in a little while."

She raised up and looked at him, brushing back his hair,
letting her fingers stay threaded through the thick dark
strands. "Why not stay? It's a long way back to your ranch.
You would do better to go in the morning when it's light."

"First, my truck is parked out front. Not so good, right?"

She shrugged. She was not going to let small-town gossip influence her life. Dropping a kiss on his lips, she lay
back against him again.

"And two?"

"Second—"

The silence went on a long time.

"Second, what?" she asked.

"I usually don't stay the night," he murmured, stroking her soft skin.

"Um, not since Alissa, right?" Caitlin was proud her voice didn't shake. She was jealous of a woman he had lost four years ago! She didn't like the feeling, but wished instead he loved her as he had once loved Alissa.

"Not since Alissa. She and I were high school sweethearts. She was the only girl for me for almost all my life."

She reared back at that and stared at him in surprise. "You're kidding!"

"Nope."

"Wow, no wonder you were angry when she and Sam had to get married. You had waited all those years…" Caitlin trailed off.

"Yeah, we'd waited to get married until I was established, and then she and Sam rushed right into it."

Another blow. Wishing she could absorb all the hurt he'd suffered, she tightened her hold and kissed him. She loved this man. Didn't know how she was so certain, but she felt it deep within her heart. And where would it get her? He'd been hurt in the past—would he ever trust again?

For tonight, it was enough that he was here with her.

"If you still love her, maybe—"

"I thought we had that established. I don't love her. I don't think I've loved her for a long time. It just took a while to sink in. Besides, do you think I'd be here if I cared for someone else?"

Did that mean he cared for her? She longed to ask, but was afraid of the answer. No strings—he'd made that clear.

"Well, I wish you would stay, but if you have to leave, don't wake me up. I don't want to know you're gone."

Caitlin awoke early the next morning despite her late-night activities. They had used three of Zach's condoms during the night. She couldn't imagine using six! Turning her head, she saw Zach, still fast asleep. Slowly she smiled. He'd stayed! Glancing at her clock she saw it was just past six. She had time to drift back to sleep before the alarm rang at seven. But she didn't want to. Turning slowly, careful not to disturb him, she watched him sleep. His dark lashes fanned out along the top of his cheeks. His lips were slightly parted, and she wanted to press hers against them. His tan looked dark against the white of her sheets and she wondered how much darker his face was than the rest of him.

Daringly, she eased the sheet down a little. He stirred, and she held her breath. When nothing further happened, she pushed it down a bit more. His eyes opened and he looked directly into hers.

"Good morning," she said, hoping he hadn't a clue what she'd intended.

"What time is it?"

"Just after six."

He looked out the window. Dawn was lightening the sky.

"I never stay all night," he growled.

Taking a deep breath, Caitlin reached out and touched his bare arm, letting her palm rest against his biceps. "It's okay when you're involved in an affair."

"My truck is out front for everyone in town to see."

"Fortunately everyone in town does not drive down my street this early in the morning. Anyway, I don't care. I'm not ashamed of what we are doing."

Zach rolled onto his back and stacked his hands beneath his head. "I must be losing my mind. Give me a second, and I'll get up and dress and be out of your way."

"Stay for breakfast, it's only English muffins and cheese. But that can tide you over until your get home and can fix a huge breakfast like I'm sure hardworking cowboys always eat."

"What time do you have to leave for school?"

"About quarter to eight."

He smiled and rolled up on one elbow to reach for her.

He'd been a damn fool, Zach fumed as he pushed the truck hard along the highway. He should have been at the ranch for chow. Now there'd be speculation as to where he'd been. If Sam or the men heard he'd gone to the school open house, they'd know instantly where he'd spent the night.

How could he have stayed the entire night with Caitlin? He never remained all night. He'd made it a rule—then caught himself. She was right—the rules were different when one entered into an affair.

Bypassing his place, he drove straight to the barn. Two of the men had horses saddled and were mounting up. He didn't see Sam, but that meant nothing. He could be inside the barn.

"Hey, Zach, missed you at breakfast," Pedro said as he vaulted into the corral to get his horse.

"Slept late. You going to check the water hole over by Bradshaws?"

"Si, then a quick tally of the cattle near there. Should be fine, we haven't had any bad weather for a while."

"Seen Sam?"

"He said something about some damned report he had to work on, so try the office."

Zach nodded and leaned against the truck. He needed to stop by the house and change. He didn't want to get his new jeans broken in this early. He'd left the bolo tie off this morning after his shower at Caitlin's, but still looked duded up. Sam could wait. With a bit of luck, he would never guess where Zach had been. Though if Caitlin had her way, the entire county would know before long.

Torn between anger, amusement and pride, he headed back for his place. The woman was a danger. She had the bit between her teeth, no doubt about it. And was as reckless as a new-broke filly. But it felt good to have a woman care enough about him to defy her better sense. As long as he didn't let down his guard, this might work. But no getting involved deeply. When she tired of the game and moved on, he'd let her go without a backward look.

And maybe if he told himself that enough times, he'd believe it!

Caitlin was on edge. Given the right circumstances she felt she could fly above Tumbleweed and soar with eagles. She smiled at odd moments during the school day, impatient for it to end. Would Zach come to see her tonight? She'd like that, but after last night, he might wait until tomorrow. Then they could go dancing again or see a movie or go out to eat. She couldn't wait!

The phone rang as she was cooking dinner. She switched off the stove and raced to answer it.

"Caitlin?"

"Hi, Zach." Smiling, she sat in the chair. "I was hoping you might stop by tonight." She surprised herself with her boldness. Almost giddy with happiness, she longed to see him again.

"I think I better stick closer to home tonight. We have a mare ready to foal. But I can take off tomorrow night. Want to go dancing?"

"Yes."

"There's a nice place in San Angelo. Wouldn't take too long to drive over there. And we can get dinner or something, too."

"What about the Oasis? I like the music they play, and I'm getting good at the Texas two-step. We could always shoot some pool if you wanted. Best two out of three. Winner gets to decide the prize." She felt positively brazen but she suspected women had been flirting like she was doing for ages. Only for her it was a first.

He hesitated.

"Zach?"

"The place in San Angelo is nice, and we could always stay over and see the town on Saturday."

Something about the tone in his voice warned her.

"You know what I think? I think you don't want to be seen in town with me. Is that it?"

"It's not that I don't want to be seen with you—"

"Puh-lease don't tell me you are worried about my reputation one more time or I'll scream! I'm all grown-up. Why does that fact seem to escape people's notice? First my parents, then Joan, now you. If you are ashamed to be seen with me, then say so, otherwise let me decide for myself what is right for me or not. And I am damned proud to be seen with you! When you decide what you want, call me."

Caitlin slammed down the phone. She was furious. Just when she thought things might start going her way, he acted like he was some kind of pariah and became noble on her to protect her.

Did all men act that way? She'd have to ask— For a moment her mind went blank. Ordinarily she'd ask her mother. Sighing softly, she wondered if she'd made a mess of her life in less than two months. Before Christmas everything has been going along smoothly. Of course she'd been completely sheltered. But she'd been fairly content when she'd thought she still was ill.

Now everything was topsy-turvy. And she had no one to blame but herself.

Although she thought she could blame Zach a bit, too. He'd worked hard to alienate himself from everyone, now he wanted to change that but was sure going about it wrong in her book.

The phone rang.

"This is Caitlin, leave a message," she said.

"You don't have an answering machine. And you're

right, I'm damned proud to be seen with you. You're an
adult, if you want to ruin your reputation, have at it. I'll
pick you up tomorrow at seven, and well have dinner in
town and then dance at the Oasis.'' He hung up.

Twirling around the room in glee, Caitlin headed back
for the kitchen to finish preparing her dinner.

Eleven

Caitlin dressed in a denim skirt and her lacy top for her date with Zach. She scooped up her hair to keep it off her neck, but let tendrils frame her face. Ready long before he was due to show up, she paced, excited to see him, worried that he'd change his mind about continuing their affair.

When she saw his truck pull up in front of the old house, she dashed down the stairs, not waiting another minute to see him.

He was halfway up the walk when she burst from the house, then teetered trying to regain her balance and walk more decorously.

"Hi," she called, her face lighting up when she saw him.

"Hi, yourself." His gaze roamed over her, from the femininity of her hairstyle to the long denim skirt. He finished just when she stopped in front of him.

"You look pretty," he said, leaning down to kiss her.

Caitlin caught her breath, stunned each time he kissed her. Each time seemed better than the last.

"I take it you're ready?" he asked a minute later.

"Been waiting for hours!" she exaggerated, tucking her hand in the crook of his arm and leaning against him. He was hers. For the duration of the affair, he was her man, and she would take advantage of every facet of that relationship. She'd waited years to have a steady boyfriend. Now she'd discover what she'd missed as a teenager.

Dinner was lighthearted and fun. Zach gently teased her, and Caitlin loved it. She took note of his every expression, his every joke and stored them up to remember later. Laughing, she leaned forward one time and caught a glimpse of pure delight in his gaze. She hoped it was due directly to her!

By the time they arrived at the cowboy bar, it was crowded. Friday nights were always popular, and the band had already begun to crank out the loud, pumping music. Caitlin moved with the beat as they threaded through the packed parking lot. Zach caught her hand and danced her the last few yards. Laughing, she knew the happiness that welled up within her matched nothing she'd ever known before. Life was so *good!*

Inside, he wasted no time in pulling her onto the dance floor. They finished the song, and when the next one was slow, Zach wrapped his arms around her and pulled her close.

"I like the slow ones the best," he murmured in her ear, giving her a light kiss.

"Me, too," she agreed, her heart racing and her mind focused only on Zach, on the feel of his long body against hers, on the sensations that rocked her very core. She loved him and cherished every moment spent in his presence. Their affair might end, but she'd have memories to treasure her entire life.

When a cowboy tapped Zach's shoulder to cut in, Zach spun her around and shook his head to the man. "Sorry, friend, this one's taken."

"Can you do that?" Caitlin asked a minute later, watching the cowboy break in on another couple.

"Just did."

"I know that, but I wondered if it were proper."

He pulled back a bit to look at her. "And if it isn't? Aren't you the original Miss Improper?"

She smiled and nodded. "Guess I am."

"Did you want to dance with him?" Zach asked.

"No. Just wondered, that's all. I like dancing with you."

Four more songs and the band took a break. Weaving their way through the crowd, Zach parried the ribald comments thrown his way. He frowned once or twice, but continued leading Caitlin toward the bar.

"I knew it would be bad," he said at one point.

She peeped at him from beneath her lashes, flirting for all she was worth. "I'm flattered, actually. And still having fun."

He looked at her and shook his head. "You are one strange woman."

"No, just someone looking to spread her wings a bit."

"And how high do you want to fly?"

"As high as you can take me, Air Force jockey."

He stopped, still a dozen steps from the bar. "So we leave now?"

She shook her head and laughed. "Not on your life! I want to have fun on this date before we go home."

"And we wouldn't have fun at home?"

Turning to the bar, she threw him a look over her shoulder. "Maybe," she teased.

"Hello, darlin'." Sam Haller stepped from the bar and greeted Caitlin.

She stopped abruptly, her smile fading. "Hi, Sam."

"Step up, I'm buying," he said to his brother, his gaze flickering between Zach and Caitlin.

"That's a switch," Zach said, putting his arm around Caitlin's shoulders in a proprietary way.

"You come with this washed-up flyboy?" Sam asked.

"I'm here with Zach," Caitlin answered quietly, feeling the tension rise between the two men. She didn't want to be in the middle. Smiling politely at Sam she said, "I'll take a cola. But I bet Zach wants a long-neck."

"A cola? Darlin' everybody in Texas drinks beer. You can't want a sissy cola. I'll order you up a beer."

Nothing guaranteed Caitlin's ire more than to be told what to do. She stepped closer and glared at him. "I do not want a beer. I want a cola!"

Sam moved back a step and stared at her. "Yes ma'am. I hear you."

Zach chuckled and Sam glanced his way, scowling. "You want a cola, too?" he asked almost sneering.

"Long-neck'll do." Zach released Caitlin. "I'm going to make a pit stop. Be right back."

"Okay."

When the cola came, she sipped it, glad for the quenching cold. She turned around to gaze out over the crowded room, hoping Zach wouldn't be too long.

"So, Caitlin, how do you like Tumbleweed now that you've been here a few weeks," Sam asked.

"I like it a lot." She took another sip and looked at him.

The band started playing again and Sam took her glass. "Come on and dance one dance while you wait for Zach. This is a great song."

She wanted to protest, but thought better of it. One dance wouldn't hurt, and maybe she could talk to Sam about his brother. Still holding on to the thought that families should be supportive, maybe she could say something to sway Sam into behaving better toward Zach. At the very least, she could let him know she knew the reputation his brother enjoyed was false.

But Sam had other ideas. "You like children, I expect, since you teach first grade."

"Yes I do," Caitlin said as they swung into a slow dance. She tried to keep a respectable distance between them, but he hugged her tightly as they moved to the music.

"I have a three-year-old son I'm working to get custody of. At least partial custody. Greg's a cute kid. And horse crazy."

"Does he ride at three?" she asked, remembering her one adventure on a horse. She'd been scared half the time. How would a three-year-old cope?

"Not yet, except up with me. But if he comes to the ranch part of the year, he'll be riding by the time he's five I expect."

"You must miss him."

"I sure do. Alissa doesn't come to the ranch at all, and it's hard for me to get away. I have to run the place you know."

"Zach could help."

"Nope."

"Why not?"

"I don't want to discuss Zach. I thought you could give me some pointers about Greg. The case comes up in court soon, and I really think I have a chance of having him at least half the time. He'll inherit my share of the ranch so I want him to know how to run it."

Caitlin smiled politely and nodded. That made sense. Glancing around, she looked to see if Zach had returned. She didn't see him.

Sam tightened his hold and spun them around. Caitlin laughed, feeling like a kid. "Tell me more about Greg," she invited.

For the rest of the dance, Sam complied. Whatever his faults, he seemed to adore his son, Caitlin thought as she listened, captivated by the antics of the small boy as proudly related by his father.

"I have a picture in the truck, want to see it?" Sam asked as the music ended.

Caitlin hesitated just a moment, but he picked up on it.

"Of course if you have just been being polite listening to me, I understand. Forget it."

"No, of course I'd like to see him." She glanced around

the room, but the crowd near the bar was six deep. She didn't see Zach. "We can come right back inside and find Zach," she said.

"Sure." He put his arm across her shoulder and headed for the door. In seconds they were in the parking lot. Sam's truck was parked in the opposite direction of Zach's and they arrived in only a minute. He opened the door, rummaged around in a pile of paper and withdrew a photograph. Holding it beneath the dome light he motioned to Caitlin. She leaned in, conscious of Sam's closeness, but she wanted to see the picture and get back inside.

"This was taken a month ago. Alissa just sent it."

Greg was adorable, Caitlin thought. He looked a lot like his daddy—and his uncle. For a moment she wondered how Zach stood seeing the son that could have been his, realizing the anguish he must have gone through when he'd found out about his brother and his fiancée.

"What the hell are you doing?" Zach asked behind them.

Sam dropped the picture, put his arm around Caitlin's shoulders and held her toward Zach. "What do you think?" Tightening his arm, he drew Caitlin closer.

She pushed against the man, pressing her hands on his chest, trying to break his hold. "Let me go!"

"Too, late, darlin', we've been discovered."

"Let me go!" She stomped her boot onto his. The pain caused his hold to relax enough for her to tear herself from his arms. She stepped back beside the truck, keeping a wary eye on Sam. As she looked quickly at Zach, her heart sank. He was furious.

"We came out—"

"I don't much care why you came out. See whomever you damn well want to. Maybe Sam will take you home and give you some more of that experience you're always going on about." Zach spun around and strode across the parking lot.

"Zach, wait!" She ran after him, but Sam caught her arm and held on.

"Let me go!" she said, struggling against his grip. When she heard Zach's truck start, she stopped struggling, watching in disbelief as he peeled out of the parking lot, the back of the truck shimmying as he accelerated. In only seconds the sound of the engine had faded.

Turning, Caitlin swung her arm and slapped Sam with all she had. Stunned, he released his grip and stepped back to lean against the truck, his hand immediately coming to his cheek.

"You bastard. You set me up!" Caitlin said, fury shaking her voice.

"I don't know what you're talking about," he denied, but the wary look in his eyes gave him away.

"I do. It wasn't enough to take Alissa away. The first time he shows an interest in another woman, you have to move in. When I wouldn't cooperate, you devised a tricky means. I bet you have a dozen pictures of Greg in your wallet. We didn't have to come out here."

"You came of your own free will. No one forced you," he said.

"Do you think he went home?" she asked, almost shaking, her anger was so great.

"I don't know. Probably." Sam stood away from the truck, ready to close the door.

"Then you can take me there," Caitlin said.

"I'm not ready to go home."

"Tough. You drive, or I'll take your truck."

"No one messes with my truck."

"Then you drive. But don't talk to me. Don't touch me, and maybe you'll get out of this alive."

The ride seemed endless. Caitlin's anger ping-ponged between Sam and Zach. Sam for his blatant attempt to drive a wedge between her and Zach, and Zach for not giving her the chance to explain. She wasn't sure which brother was more stubborn, but she had had enough.

Zach's truck was in front of his house, and Sam stopped behind it. "You're here."

"Get out," she ordered, throwing open her door and marching up to the front door. She banged with her fist. Caitlin had never been so angry in her life. The adrenaline pouring through her gave her strength and determination. Even when she'd discovered the perfidy of her parents she had not been this mad. Maybe because the stakes had not been as high.

Zach opened the door. "What do you want?" he asked, looking beyond her to Sam.

"To talk to you, both of you." Caitlin crossed the porch to stand at the steps and looked from one to another.

"I've had it up to my back teeth trying to understand you, Zach Haller. Trying to show you that I care about you. Well, you've just proved to me that you don't want what is right beneath your nose. So be it. But maybe it's time you learned a few things. First is how to fight for what you want. Expecting everything to go your way is dumb. Life is just not like that. But to roll over and play dead at the first sign of controversy is stupid. You'll never get anything that way."

"Maybe he—" Sam started to speak.

"You shut up. I'm the one talking here," she said, turning her head to glare at him. "You're as much at fault with your underhanded ways as he is for giving in to them. You stole his fiancée. Can you imagine what that would do to a man—his brother stealing his fiancée? The two people in the world he probably love the most betraying him? And when he was away from home and unable to do anything about it. I think that's the lowest thing I ever heard."

"Caitlin," Zach said.

"I'm the one talking!" She took a deep breath. "You think you're being so noble, pretending you don't care about anything, letting everything roll off your back. But that's not being noble, that's caving in. That's giving in to the hard knocks of life, and it isn't right. I love you, Zach

Haller. I think I have since that first night I met you. But you blow hot then cold. I can't tell if you like me or just want my body. If you really liked me, you'd want to spend time with me.''

''What do you think I've been doing?''

''You've been telling me since the very beginning that you are not interested. No ties, no string, no nothing! Doesn't sound very interested in me at all.''

''Should have listened to his reputation, Caitlin, that would have given you the first clue,'' Sam interjected.

She glared at Sam and took the two steps down to the ground. ''Zach's reputation is a myth,'' she said firmly.

''What?''

''That's right, and I suspect it's been deliberately fostered to keep people from the truth.''

''Caitlin,'' Zach warned.

''What truth?'' Sam asked at the same time.

''The truth about how he felt about you and Alissa, and about what your father did. You all were a family. Isn't family supposed to stick together, no matter what? To support each other, help each other, be there for each other? But your family practices betrayal. And it's not fair. Do you know he has a ton of books on cattle and ranch management he's studying, because he didn't take those courses in college? He wants to learn all he can about ranching, since that's what he's doing now.''

''Caitlin, that's enough, I can fight my own battles,'' Zach came down the steps and took her shoulders in his hands, facing her and glaring down into her face.

''That's just it, Zach, you don't. You let your brother get away with everything, and hide behind a devil-may-care mask that everyone else is starting to believe. Don't you care enough about me to fight for me? Even for an affair? I love you. I want you in my life. I don't think that's asking so much, is it? I haven't had much in twenty-four years, but I know real gold when I see it, and you're that. Only you won't even meet me halfway!''

"It's just—"

"I don't want to hear any excuses. Either do or don't do. But don't keep talking about it."

She pulled away from him and stormed over to his truck. If she didn't get away soon, she would burst into tears and make a total fool of herself. The key was in the ignition. She climbed in and started it.

"Don't take my truck," Zach roared, but she ignored him and started for town. By the time she reached the highway the tears were falling so fast she could hardly see. But she dashed them away. She was going home and—

She didn't know what she was going to do, but apparently she would be doing it alone.

Zach pulled Sam's truck to the curb behind his own. Sunlight glinted on the windows. The morning breeze blew against his cheeks as he climbed out, turning to look at Pedro as the man slid across the seat to the driver's position. "Get those fasteners at the hardware, would you before you head back to the ranch?"

"Sure, boss." Pedro grinned at him and closed the door.

As the truck drove off, Zach walked to his. His key was not inside. Slowly he smiled, then winced. At least she had to see him, if only to return the key. Satisfied, he turned and started up the walk. Glancing up at her windows, he thought he saw the curtain move, but wasn't sure.

Knocking on her door a moment later, he took off his hat and ran his fingers through his hair. He was nervous. Damn, he couldn't believe it.

She opened the door and he forgot what he wanted to say. Caitlin Delany was the most beautiful woman he'd ever seen. He'd known it from the first. Had he told her?

"Oh, Zach, what happened?" Her eyes widened with surprise, then softened into compassion as she reached out to lightly brush her fingertips across the bruise by his eye.

"Can I come in?" He caught her hand and kissed the

palm, folding it in his and holding on tightly so she couldn't pull away.

"Of course." She stepped aside so he could enter. Zach closed the door and pulled her gently into his arms.

"I love you, Caitlin," he said just before his mouth came down on hers. For a second he thought she was not going to respond, but then she did, gloriously giving in her kisses, her arms tight around his neck as if she'd never let go. Slowly the fear eased, his nervousness faded. The awful blackness in his soul eased, and sunlight sparkled.

"Wow!" she said when he broke the kiss.

He smiled and rested his head carefully against hers. "I like 'wow!'"

"I'm not sure I heard you correctly a moment ago, want to repeat it?"

"I love you, Caitlin Delany," he said softly. His eyes looked deeply into hers. "I knew it last night when I saw you with Sam in the parking lot. For one awful moment I thought history was repeating itself. That the woman I wasn't even willing to admit I loved was turning to my brother. With that searing thought, I realized I loved you more than anything. Much more than I ever did Alissa."

"So you cut and ran?"

"More like retreated to lick my wounds, and tried to sort through the emotions that I found. You have to understand that I thought I'd go through life alone after Alissa turned from me. I never expected this. But I love you, Caitlin. And after your shouting on the porch last night, I think you feel the same."

"I love you, too, Zach Haller."

He tightened his hold on her. "I hoped you meant it after you told me and the entire world last night."

"I told you I wasn't ashamed of anything. I'm feeling pretty damned proud at this moment if you want to know the truth. I knew when you tore out of that parking lot last night that you were the only one for me. Maybe we should both thank your brother."

"Good grief, your head is going to swell so big when I tell you what's happened, I won't be able to stand it."

"Me? I'll have you know, Mr. Haller, my mother raised a lady. I would never get a big head. Or at least never brag about it. What happened? And how did you get a black eye?"

He drew her over to the sofa and sat down, tugging until she sat beside him. Wearily Zach leaned his head back. It pounded a bit. Maybe he needed more aspirin.

"Tell me," she repeated.

"Sam and I got into a fight after you left. Verbal at first, but when he—"

"When he what?" she prodded when he paused.

"When it got a little too mouthy about you, I punched him. He came back."

"I don't believe in this day and age cowboys still fight."

"Yeah, well I can believe it. I have the bruises to prove it."

"And did it settle anything?"

He looked at her ceiling, then dropped his gaze to her face, smiling. "Yeah, it settled a lot. Are you going to marry me?"

"What? Marry you?"

"Isn't that usually what two people in love do?"

"I guess. You want to marry me? What about no strings? No commitment?"

"I'm fighting for what I want now," he said. "And I want you. Today, tomorrow and forever."

"Well, cowboy, I reckon I can say a mighty big yes to that."

He groaned. "Honey, don't pick up a Texas drawl, stick with your Southern charm."

She laughed and hugged him. "I love you, Zach. I would truly be so honored to marry you. I can't believe you asked me."

"You were right last night. I thought I was being so noble after all that happened. In reality I was covering up how I felt, and letting everyone get off scot-free for what was really their doing."

"So you settled things with Sam?"

"You could say so. He's leaving."

"What?"

"He's going to Denver for a long visit. To talk with Alissa and to see Greg. Then he's going to travel a little before coming home."

"And in the meantime?"

"In the meantime, I'm running the place. And Sam's offered me enough of his share in the ranch that we'll each have a fifty-fifty split."

"Will it stand up in court?"

"What?" Zach looked at her puzzled.

"Your coercing him into giving you a bigger share."

"That's not what we fought over. And it was his idea, so I don't think there will be a problem."

"What did you fight over?"

"You, mainly. But it felt good to get a few punches in for the last few years, I have to tell you." They'd also fought over Alissa, and cleared the air on that issue, but he didn't think it wise to discuss that with Caitlin just yet. Time enough to tell her everything when she felt sure of his love. As sure as he felt about it.

She smiled and lightly brushed his swollen eye. "I'm not worth fighting over, but I'm secretly thrilled you did. I've never had a man fight over me."

He took a deep breath. "I know. In fact you are the most innocent woman I know."

When she started to protest, he raised his hand. "Wait a minute. I know what you're going to say, but hear me out. I'm talking this time. Since you've been here in Tumbleweed, you've been spreading your wings to fly. But it's all new to you. And you might think this is great, but there are a lot of men out there, Caitlin, many you haven't met. I want you, I love you and I'll about die if you don't want me back in the same way, but I could not stand for you to change your mind in a few years and want out.''

''I'm not going to change my mind. I may not have the experience you do, but I know my own mind and my heart. And I have the example of my parents for a loving long-term marriage.''

''Are you sure?''

''I'm sure. Are we going to have lots of babies?''

''Right now all I want is you. But if you want babies, I guess we can.''

''Greg needs cousins, and my folks need grandbabies before they get much older.''

''About your folks—''

Her fingertips covered his lips. ''Shh. I was going to tell you. I called them this morning. We had a great talk and cleared the air. You were right, they love me. And I miss them.''

''Don't you feel better?''

''I should warn you right now, I don't like I-told-you-so's!''

He laughed and hugged her tightly, his hands already following the curves of her body. His blood thundered in his veins and he wondered how much longer he could talk. He wanted to make love to her so badly he ached!

''We'll have a lot to learn about each other once we're married,'' he murmured.

''At least this should put paid to your bad reputation. Won't our marriage surprise everyone? Oh, what about Margot?''

''I told Sam I never slept with her. He knows he's the father, but he doesn't remember that night too clearly, just moving in on her when she and I were flirting, to get back at me. He's going over to talk to her this morning. He doesn't love her, but he's going to provide for the child.''

''Did he love Alissa?'' she asked.

He looked at her for a long moment. So much for keeping anything from her. Slowly he nodded. ''He says so.

Said he loved her all along. Had to make a move when she started planning our wedding. I don't know, Caitlin. I can't decide if he really wanted her, or just wanted to get back at me. Seems like he never wanted to run the ranch, but couldn't step out from under Dad's thumb. All his life he was pushed as the older son. He envied me and resented me. I can't believe I never saw it as a kid.''

"Teenagers don't see anything but themselves. He had years to get over that resentment. Have you two really worked things out?''

"Time will tell. But I think we can work together in the future. We spent half the night talking and patching each other up. He's taking some time to find what he really wants in life. And I've decided ranching isn't the worst thing I could do. We'll see when he gets back, but I truly think we might manage. And I'll have you with me, right?''

"Every step of the way, Zach. I'll love you forever.''

"Good,'' he said with deep satisfaction. "Because that's about as long as I plan to love you, sweetheart.''

Caitlin's heart swelled to overflowing when her cowboy drew her into his arms for another kiss. Together they would share a lifetime of kisses, love and happiness!

*   *   *   *   *

You won't want to miss this wonderful author's next book, TRIAL ENGAGEMENT, *available from Harlequin Romance in September 1999. Look for Barbara McMahon's exciting debut in Silhouette Special Edition this November!*

SILHOUETTE®

Desire®

May '99
LOVE ME TRUE
#1213 by ANN MAJOR

June '99
THE STARDUST COWBOY
#1219 by Anne McAllister

July '99
PRINCE CHARMING'S CHILD
#1225 by Jennifer Greene

August '99
THAT BOSS OF MINE
#1231 by Elizabeth Bevarly

September '99
LEAN, MEAN & LONESOME
#1237 by Annette Broadrick

October '99
FOREVER FLINT
#1243 by Barbara Boswell

MAN of the **Month**

MAN OF THE MONTH

For ten years Silhouette Desire
has been giving readers the ultimate in sexy,
irresistible heroes. Come join the celebration as some
of your favorite authors help celebrate our
anniversary with the most sensual, emotional love
stories ever!

Available at your favorite retail outlet.

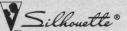

Silhouette®

If you enjoyed what you just read,
then we've got an offer you can't resist!

Take 2 bestselling love stories FREE!
Plus get a FREE surprise gift!

Clip this page and mail it to Silhouette Reader Service™

IN U.S.A.
3010 Walden Ave.
P.O. Box 1867
Buffalo, N.Y. 14240-1867

IN CANADA
P.O. Box 609
Fort Erie, Ontario
L2A 5X3

YES! Please send me 2 free Silhouette Desire® novels and my free surprise gift. Then send me 6 brand-new novels every month, which I will receive months before they're available in stores. In the U.S.A., bill me at the bargain price of $3.12 plus 25¢ delivery per book and applicable sales tax, if any*. In Canada, bill me at the bargain price of $3.49 plus 25¢ delivery per book and applicable taxes**. That's the complete price and a savings of over 10% off the cover prices—what a great deal! I understand that accepting the 2 free books and gift places me under no obligation ever to buy any books. I can always return a shipment and cancel at any time. Even if I never buy another book from Silhouette, the 2 free books and gift are mine to keep forever. So why not take us up on our invitation. You'll be glad you did!

225 SEN CNFA
326 SEN CNFC

Name	(PLEASE PRINT)	
Address	Apt.#	
City	State/Prov.	Zip/Postal Code

* Terms and prices subject to change without notice. Sales tax applicable in N.Y.
** Canadian residents will be charged applicable provincial taxes and GST.
   All orders subject to approval. Offer limited to one per household.
   ® are registered trademarks of Harlequin Enterprises Limited.

DES99   ©1998 Harlequin Enterprises Limited